BAKERTON

Phil Clinker

BAKERTON

Pegasus

PEGASUS PAPERBACK

© Copyright 2019
Phil Clinker

A CIP catalogue record for this title is
available from the British Library

ISBN: 978 1 910903 2 78

*Pegasus is an imprint of
Pegasus Elliot MacKenzie Publishers Ltd.*
www.pegasuspublishers.com

First Published in 2019

**Pegasus
Sheraton House Castle Park
Cambridge CB3 0AX England**

Printed & Bound in Great Britain

To my darling wife of 48 years,
Olive,
with all my love

The contiguous towns of Copper Ridge, Thurlow Junction and Bakerton form what the locals refer to as 'The Triangle'. Copper Ridge came first, of course, created out of the lumber sites set up in the late 1860s, when the abundant copper birch trees were felled to make canoes and roof trusses for buildings. Twenty years later, the railway authorities built a junction in the valley immediately below the Ridge, believing that the great age of the copper birch was still to come. They were wrong. Although the tiny hamlet of Thurlow grew up around the junction, the timber trade fell away sharply by the turn of the twentieth century and the junction itself became obsolete, forming now a mere backdrop to the increasingly cosmopolitan little town of Thurlow Junction.

In 1920, Hiram Baker bought a huge tract of land to the west of Thurlow from the rail company. Baker had been almost physically destroyed by the Great War, and it was his intention to develop a new town where like people could recover and live in peace. The fact that he was a multi-millionaire through inheritance meant that the people he attracted were also well-heeled, so Bakerton began life as a playboy's haven. Firstly, Baker constructed the Western Lake, the largest mass of blue most people had ever seen, and built his mansion beside it, as far away from Thurlow Junction as he could get. His friends did likewise, and by the 1930s the little town was ticking over very nicely, thank you.

However, life does not go on, and Hiram Baker died in 1953, leaving the town – and the vast tract of unused no-man's-land to the east – to his sons, both of whom were business graduates with an eye to the bottom line. It took them less than two years to start selling off small chunks of the land for development, and within a short time, the town of Bakerton was firmly on the map as *the* place to be for middle-class families looking for peace and tranquillity and a 'rural' outlook.

Now, although the town no longer has a rural aspect, due to the number of buildings squashed into the land, it still has its reputation…

Nothing *ever* happens in Bakerton.

DAY ONE

Chapter One

The three men crept slowly through the house. Only one of them had been there before, but they knew exactly where they were going. They were in single-file, the leader holding his right hand high, his fingers making almost imperceptible movements of command to the other men. They were all dressed the same: black jogging pants, black sweatshirts, black gloves and black balaclavas, so only their eyes were visible. They each held a weapon, with silencer, and the short, stocky Number Three also had a machete in a scabbard slung over his back.

The leader's finger twitched, and the men stopped in perfect unison. A well-drilled team. The finger was then crooked, so the men crouched, silent, awaiting unspoken instructions. They all knew that if the enemy suddenly appeared and began firing, they would aim for the head and upper torso, the bullets thus flying over their crouching bodies. At least, that was the theory.

The leader's balaclava was being sucked in and out as he breathed himself to steadiness. He had learnt many years ago the art of control – both physical and cerebral. When his breathing was sufficiently calm, he looked again at their situation.

They were in a hallway, its wooden flooring polished and smooth. He vaguely noticed a couple of large pictures on one wall, garish in colour and not at all to his taste. There was a crystal tear-drop chandelier, of all things, suspended from the vaulted ceiling, emphasising the opulence of the place. Beautiful timber rafters kept the roof in place, their polished burnt umber colour contrasting with the white-painted walls. It was altogether an impressive home, one fit for a king. Or a banker.

But the thing the leader couldn't understand was the *silence*. He had expected some kind of opposition; a sign that they were expecting him. Perhaps, after all this time, they really *did* believe he was dead. Fools!

There was a door to the left, but he ignored it, knowing it led only to a dining room and beyond that a conservatory opening out to the beautifully landscaped gardens and a drive sweeping out to the highway a quarter of a mile away. He had considered this door a secondary escape route should they meet opposition, but it was clear that was not going to be necessary. It was all so easy.

****

There had been an air of bonhomie, but now the three other men fell silent as the chairman of the bank rose to address them. He was solemn and serious, as befitted a man of his position.

He cleared his throat. "My friends, thank you for coming today. It has been a while since we had a meeting like this, but I wanted to get you together for what will probably be the last time."

There was a ripple of concern from the others, but the chairman continued, "I will not dwell on past misfortune, only to say thank you for your support during a very difficult time for all of us."

"We're always here for you!" one of the others said, and the room became awash with good humour.

The chairman raised an arm. "I am honoured, gentlemen… but I fear that, while you will always be here for me, I cannot say the same." He watched their faces, all banter long gone. This was going to be serious, and he could see they weren't sure how to react. He gave them a thin smile. "My friends, you are the first to know… I have terminal cancer. I have only a matter of weeks to live." The silence was stunning. "I shall inform the bank tomorrow and will take a leave of absence – for as long as I am able. What you might call gardening leave, perhaps." His attempt at humour fell on deaf ears, everyone too shaken by the announcement. After all they had been through…

****

The finger flexed, and the men inched forward to the door in front of them. The leader could hear voices now, deep in conversation. The door was, like the rest of the house, built of solid oak, so the sounds were muffled, and they could only guess at what was being said; although the leader knew exactly who was beyond that door and why they were there. He was well informed.

The leader indicated for his Number Two to come forward and motioned to the door handle. They stood either side of the door, with Number Three holding back a little, just in case. Again, a well-drilled team.

Number Two turned the handle and threw the door open. It wasn't as smooth an operation as they had hoped, because the door was heavy and the carpet in the room was deep. With the door stopping halfway, the leader had to lean into it to gain entrance, so his arrival was not as professional as he had intended. Even so, the men in the room had no time to react before they had three pistols trained on them as the visitors fanned out and surveyed the scene.

"What the…?" began the chairman, rising and leaning on the table.

The leader waved his pistol. "Sit down, Leroy." The chairman froze. "I said sit down, Leroy. All of you."

They obeyed, meekly.

The leader looked at them one by one, recognising them all. "Well, well, a full house – *almost*. So, Leroy, you're planning your next adventure, right?"

"If only," Leroy sighed heavily. Regaining a certain amount of composure, he said, "Who are you? And how do you know me?"

The leader grinned, although they could not see it. "I know you all, Leroy."

"Who are you?" Leroy repeated, this time a little more concerned. He was a rich and powerful man, but he never dreamt that he could have powerful enemies, and he had certainly never expected anything like this. A thought suddenly came to him. "What have you done with my housekeeper? If you've harmed…"

Another wave of the leader's pistol. "The little lady down the corridor, you mean. So sad."

Incensed, Leroy made a move to stand up. "What have you done…?"

Number Two stepped forward and brought the butt of his pistol down hard on Leroy's hand, which he was using to lever himself out of the chair.

"Do I have to tell you again, Leroy? Sit down – there's a good dog," said the leader, chuckling at his own comment. "Good dog."

There was a long silence as the men at the table looked at each other with a mixture of confusion and fear, while the leader studied each one in turn, enjoying the power he held over them. Finally, he spoke.

"Baxter," he said, looking at the youngest and most timid of them, "kindly stand up and go in the corner over there." He indicated the furthest point from the table, next to the drinks cabinet, which the leader had not seen earlier. "Ah, all mod cons, eh, Leroy? Pour me a drink, will you, Baxter?"

Baxter stood by the cabinet, amazed that the intruder knew his name and unsure of how to proceed. His voice was high-pitched and wavering. "What would you like, sir?"

The three masked men laughed in unison. "Sir!" chuckled Number Two. "I love it." He had some kind of an accent, Baxter thought. Was it familiar?

The leader crossed the room and stood next to Baxter, his balaclava almost touching the other man's nose. Their eyes locked, with Baxter blinking madly, and the sweat pouring off him almost dripped onto the man who was threatening him. "You know what I like, Baxter," the leader said simply.

"I do?"

"Oh, yes you do. You all do." He looked around again, his eyes closing in on the man at the head of the table. "Don't you, Leroy?"

Everyone waited for a response, but Leroy's mind was in turmoil. He was sure he recognised the voice, but there were no outward signs he could see that would indicate his visitor's identity. What the fuck was going on here? Some wise-guy with a couple of heavies had forced his way into Leroy's house, done whatever to Mrs Gonzalez, and now were intent on... again, who knew what? Leroy took a deep breath, gathering his thoughts. "Tell me who you are, and I'll tell you what you drink," he said, his voice coming out stronger than he had ever hoped. It was time he took control here. "Show yourself!" he ordered, his hands clenched into fists under the table, probably through panic rather than any real thought of fighting back.

The leader chuckled again, a guttural sound which carried more menace than humour. "I'll show you who I am, Leroy," he said, moving beside one of the other men seated next to Leroy. Without another word, the leader raised his pistol and shot the man through the forehead, neatly between the eyes. "Baxter," he said, "please be so kind as to sit this gentleman back upright. He seems to have slumped in his chair."

Number Two and Number Three thought this was hilarious, and both laughed heartily as Baxter, now a complete wreck, endeavoured to reposition the body. He failed miserably, so Number Two pushed him away and finished the job.

"Thank you, Number Two. I always knew Baxter was useless."

"But I…" Baxter began, but decided it was wiser not to finish, so he slinked back into the corner, tears welling in his eyes.

Leroy had watched all this with his mouth open. Now this really was serious. He had to talk this madman down before he killed them all. He couldn't work out why these people would possibly want to kill him and his colleagues. Unless… Suddenly, the truth began to emerge from the fuzz of his addled brain. No, it couldn't be. Surely he's dead… Ty killed him, what, four years ago now. Ty, the hitman… I saw him do it…

The leader could see the change on Leroy's face, and slapped Number Two on the back. "Now he remembers! Well done, Leroy, I'm proud of you. I really didn't want to finish this before we had been reacquainted." With that, he went to the other man at the table and put a bullet in him, in exactly the same place as the first one. Baxter screamed and slid to the floor, his legs giving way. He whimpered loudly, his breaths coming in jerking waves.

"Don't worry, Baxter, it'll soon be over," the leader said soothingly, as he pulled off his balaclava and gave Leroy the most horrific smile imaginable.

****

Baxter stumbled to the front door, leaving trails of blood along the hallway walls. As he looked at the red mess he was leaving behind, he was so grateful that none of it was his. He couldn't believe his good fortune.

He forced open the door and fell out into the sunshine, gasping in the fresh, crisp air of the early evening. He frantically looked around, fearing that they were still there, but he was met with the most wonderful silence he had ever experienced. He was alive!

He sat on the step, wondering how this might develop. They had told him *exactly* what to do, but he still found himself weighing up his options. He could run. He had enough money left for a very long trip overseas – say twenty years – and he could even take Salome, the whore who'd been dipping into his wallet recently. She was good at her job, and he was sure she'd tag along for the ride – or quite a few rides, he reckoned. Salome wasn't her real name, of course, but she chose it because she liked giving head, as opposed to the real one, who *took* a head. Baxter didn't understand what the hell she was talking about; but, like he said, she was *so* good at her job.

He rocked back and threw his arms around his body. He suddenly felt cold, the shivers forcing their way down his back. No, he couldn't run – they'd catch up with him for sure. And, after what he had just been a party to, he didn't want to think about what they might do to him.

No, he would have to do what they said. He reached into the breast pocket of his shirt and noticed for the first time that the blood had seeped through it, and he could feel the gooey mess matting the few chest hairs he had. He pulled out his mobile, also covered with specks of blood. There had been so much of it...

With twitching fingers, he switched on the phone and keyed-in the number. He took a great gulp of air and exhaled just as the call was answered.

The sound of another voice seemed to overwhelm him, and he broke down, the tears and gulps wracking his body. Eventually, he could just about mumble into the phone, "He's alive!"

Chapter Two

Ty Cobden was waiting at the junction of Rift Street and Hawth Place, in the east of Bakerton, a town he'd never expected to come back to. To him, it was bleak and boring beyond reason, but necessity led him here. Or, to be more precise, Ralphie Baxter had led him here.

The phone call had come out of the blue, and Ty didn't really want to believe it. Not after all this time. It was a pointer that he had slipped up big time four years ago. Something had gone terribly wrong, and now he was going to have to clear up the mess he had unwittingly created. And what a fucking mess it was, too. Hell, he wasn't on Rift Street at all – he was on Shit Street.

He eased his six-foot-four frame out of the red sports car that was his pride and joy – the only thing he owned, and it was legit, too. His features were set like granite, and his deep blue eyes were like pinpricks. He sucked in his cheeks and rubbed a hand over his stubble. He still couldn't believe that Leroy had gone.

He pulled out a holdall from the passenger seat and placed it on the wall beside him. All he could do now was wait… and contemplate.

Baxter's call had unnerved him more than he had realised. With his experience, he thought he was immune to nasty surprises, but this was just too much. *The General was back.* The bastard had survived Ty's final attack; but how was that possible? Ty had seen the body – hell, he'd put two more bullets in it, just to make sure. And now… now the Arsehole was back here in this godforsaken town, intent on revenge, and already clearing away the deadwood in his quest for the final prize: Ty Cobden, aka Lucas Black.

He took out a packet of gum and tossed a strip in his mouth, chewing intently as he thought some more. Baxter had said there were three of them, so the General had enlisted troops, and Ty knew they would be good. In that respect, Ty and the General were of the same mind – surround yourself with trustworthy and professional men. Unfortunately for Ty, though, there was no one else left. He had fought the General to the finish – but had no army. He would just have to go solo on this mission.

A car screeched to a halt beside him, Baxter jumping out almost before it had stopped.

"Ty, Ty, thank God you're here," he wailed, reaching the wall and leaning against it, exhausted. "It's a fucking nightmare, Ty; a fuc—"

"Okay, Ralphie, just take it easy. You're safe now. All you've got to do is tell me everything."

Baxter's breathing eased back, and he reached for a cigarette from his jacket pocket, then fumbled for his lighter. "Fuck! I can't find…"

Ty did not smoke, but he always carried a lighter. You never knew when it might come in handy. He lit the cigarette, and Baxter puffed heavily on it for a few seconds, slowly coming back to planet Earth. "Thanks, Ty. I need this." Ty nodded, a prompt for Baxter to continue. "It was definitely him. Him and two other fuc—"

"Recognise them?"

"No, Ty, but they were good. Just like you in the old days."

Not so old days, Ty thought, although it seemed like a lifetime ago. He had been living easy over the last four years, free from any problems, and able to drift from place to place in his car, picking up loose and not so loose women, spending the three million he'd earned. It was luck – good or bad, he wasn't sure – that saw him only an hour away from Bakerton when he got the call. He had to drop a red-hot cert likely to have made him a lot of cash, which did not please him, and take a journey back in time. Now that he was standing in the centre of this town, he wasn't a hundred percent sure what he was going to do.

"They made me... chop him up, Ty."

Baxter's voice found its way into Ty's clouded mind, and he jerked upright. "What?"

Baxter jumped back at Ty's sudden movement, his nerves shot through many times over. "The General... he made me..."

"Chop him up. Yeah, I heard you the first time. Are we talking Leroy here?"

Baxter nodded. "*Before* they killed him..." His voice trailed off at the enormity of the ordeal he had been through. "First, his hand..."

Ty recoiled. "Yeah, okay, enough." He was only just getting over the shock of losing his only friend; now Ralphie was hell-bent on embellishing his thoughts with pictures that had no place in the subconscious mind of a sane person. He didn't want to remember it all in years to come. Eventually, it seemed that, for the first time, Ty's eyes took in the blood on Baxter's hands and clothes. "Shit!" He paused. "And they let you live." It wasn't a question, just a statement of an unbelievable fact.

"Leroy didn't say a word, Ty. And I didn't tell them you were operating under a different name now. But they told me to find you, Ty, and tell you that the General is after you for what you did."

26

Baxter took a step back when he realised what he had said, and added very quickly, "His words, Ty, not mine. His…!"

"Yeah. Understood." Ty grabbed Baxter's collar and squeezed. "You did what I told you on the way here, yeah?"

Baxter was shaking. "Of course, Ty. I went around the block a few times and stopped off at the mall, like you said. I went into six shops, leaving through different doors, and around the block again. Nobody was following me, I swear."

Ty released his grip. He knew Baxter hadn't been tailed, because he had tracked him through binoculars for the last quarter mile. That's why he had picked this spot – it offered a great view to the west of the town, from which direction Baxter would be coming. He knew, but he wanted him to fry a little.

"They're all dead, Ty. There's only you and me left. We've got to stick together."

"Relax, Ralphie. Puff on your cig and take five. I need to think." Ty moved behind the wall and began to take off his jacket.

"What're you doing?" asked Baxter.

"We need to go back."

Baxter recoiled in horror. "You kidding me?"

Ty opened his holdall and removed a forensics suit with hood, gloves and bootees. As he put them on, he smiled reassuringly at Baxter. "You can stay in the car. Just take me there. I have to see for myself."

"But what's with the gear, Ty?"

"It's all right for you, because you were there, Ralphie. The cops will know that by the forensics. But I don't want to leave anything of me there. I'm just playing safe."

Baxter nodded. He knew he was going to be okay. Ty wouldn't let him down. And, besides, he didn't have to go back inside that hell-house. He was just the driver. He looked at his knuckles: they weren't as white as they had been, and his breathing was shallower and more relaxed. Wow, he thought with a relieved sigh, he had come out the other side, almost unscathed.

****

The drive back was almost fun. Ty might have looked a little stupid in that get-up, but Baxter, hands on the wheel and one arm resting on the door with the window down, was animated and almost excited. He had talked non-stop as he snaked his car round the familiar roads leading west to Leroy's house.

Four years ago, after the showdown, Baxter had gone back to Bakerton with his boss Leroy. He loved the town and the surrounding area, leasing a place up on Copper Ridge for his summer breaks and a smart little townhouse near the brothel where Salome plied her trade in Bakerton.

He needed nothing, although his share of the spoils was beginning to dwindle a little, so he might need to be careful for a while. Perhaps he wouldn't take Salome, after all. Expensive bitch!

No, he would move on somewhere nice and find a special girl to play with. Somewhere far from the General… or Ty – whichever one survived the next few days.

They had reached the turning, and Baxter swung the car into the drive, and the house came into view.

"Some place, huh?" said Baxter.

Ty nodded. "Sure is. But he's still dead."

Baxter couldn't argue with that logic, so he stayed quiet as they approached the front of the building.

"Is there a back way in?" asked Ty.

"Yeah."

"Then go round there."

Baxter did as he was told and pulled up outside the conference room where the massacre had taken place. His heart skipped several beats as he tried to look away.

"Stay in the car," ordered Ty.

"Too fucking right I am," replied Baxter, a thin smile on his face. It was a nervous reaction, because he felt far from happy, and couldn't wait for this to end. He'd soon be long gone.

Ty looked through the window at the carnage and winced. He walked slowly to the door, due to both the tension he felt and the uncomfortable protective clothing he was wearing. He turned the handle, and the door opened onto the end of a hallway. He looked to his right and saw the front door in the distance, as well as the body of a woman propped up against the wall several feet in from the door. Shit! There was no need for that. He could just see the General claiming it as collateral damage, without the slightest tinge of guilt. How Ty hated that term. *Collateral*, my arse. That was just cold-blooded murder. Another reason why Ty needed to kill this man for a second time.

To Ty's left was the door to the conference room. It was open, presumably due to the great haste Baxter was in when he left the house. Poor Baxter. He just couldn't cope. No wonder the General left him alive to tell the world what had happened. Ty was surprised Baxter hadn't soiled his pants.

Ty took a deep breath before he went into the room. He didn't want to see Leroy after what Ralphie had told him, but he had no choice. Besides, he couldn't do a damn thing for them now.

His mind could never have sufficiently forewarned him as to what he would be seeing. Poor

Leroy and the others, sitting perfectly still as if in mid-conference, only the blood and guts spread across the table and floor offering some idea of how their meeting had really ended.

Ty wasn't sure what, if anything, he was looking for. He only knew that the General had an agenda, and at the top of it was his elimination.

He passed a cursory look over each body but knew that the General wouldn't be that obvious. He looked through the drawers in the cabinet behind Leroy's decapitated corpse, under the carpet and around the radiator, finally moving to the drinks cabinet and opening the doors. There was a glass set apart from the rest with a piece of card in it. Ty took it out and held it up. As he was about to read it, he saw Baxter through the window, sitting in the car and waving breezily at him. He seemed to be over the worst now.

Ty twirled the card in his right hand and read it: *"What, no Malibu & Coke? Shame!"* Typical General, Ty thought. He flicked the card to his left hand and held it up. It read: "LUCAS BLACK", and underneath it was a single, perfect fingerprint.

It took a moment before Ty realised that the print had to be his. The General had lifted it from something he had touched; or, worse, had access to the original fingerprints on file. How was that possible?

Ty pocketed the card, took one last look round the room and left, retracing his steps to Baxter's car.

"Everything okay, Ty?" Baxter asked, seeing the thoughtful look on his face.

"Yeah," drawled Ty. "I think so, Ralphie. Just a couple of loose ends to tie up, that's all." He leant in through the driver's window, his left hand gripping the door, and smiled. "*Now* you can call the cops."

Chapter Three

Sheriff John Withers leaned back in his chair and looked out the window. The view was quite stunning, with Copper Ridge dominating the skyline and the street below him lined with trees and hanging baskets. The early evening sun was just thinking about setting, its rays turning wispy and getting weaker. Withers loved being outside, that feeling of freedom. He had been brought up in a rural village, and that had never left him. After what had happened, perhaps that was why he had jumped at the chance to transfer to sunny Bakerton, an insignificant little town with no major crime, but with the same sort of outlook and mood as his hometown. Being appointed sheriff after only two years was an added bonus.

But there was still the paperwork. Here he was, seven at night, filling in forms and filing; jobs his deputies might well have been doing, had they not gone home to their families and girlfriends. The work could have waited until the morning, but what the heck… get it done while you can, that was his dictum.

If there was a typical sheriff, Withers wasn't him. At age forty and standing a little over six feet, his black hair was longer than regulation, a slight silvery-grey tinge beginning to show itself in places, and he wore thick bifocal glasses over his sparkling hazy-green eyes. He'd tried contacts, but they made him look like a green-eyed monster, so somebody had once told him. The contacts were quickly consigned to the ophthalmologist's bin, and the 'Clark Kent' pair replaced them. With his sharp jaw, the greying medium-stubble beard and Greek nose, he would have passed for approaching handsome without the glasses… but then he wouldn't have been able to see a thing!

Withers was not what most people would call a loner. No family were left – his parents had both died before his twentieth birthday – and, of course, there had been Heather… He loved cats but felt it would be unfair to entertain the idea of offering one a home due to his job; and he had, for several years, been partnered with a Labrador-cross which ruled the roost, until old age took him. That hurt Withers almost as much as the loss of his parents.

Through the window, his eyes picked up on the Moody girl, heading home from her stint at Scotty's Diner across the street from the police station. She was an attractive sight, her long blonde hair swaying in the slight breeze which always seemed to come off the lake at this time of the year. She walked briskly, dodging a car as she crossed the road, and disappeared into Hall's Haberdashery – a posh name for a clothes shop, thought Withers. It was their late night, he knew, and she loved going in there. Millie Moody always looked presentable, and Withers made a mental note to look out for her tomorrow, just to see what item of clothing she had bought.

His interest stemmed not from any perversion or sexual orientation – hell, he was chess-playing pals with her father – but from his love of all things beautiful: from the paintings of Canaletto to the jazz guitar of Django Reinhardt. He could never understand how a man could be accepted if he studied a nude painting but was ostracised if he looked wondrously at a fully clothed young woman. The world has gone crackpot.

He pulled open his drawer and took an extra strong mint from the packet. Another ten minutes, and I'm out of here, he thought, his gaze returning to the work on his desk. Then the phone rang.

"Sheriff Withers."

"Hi…" The voice sounded agitated. "I want to report a murder… some murders."

Withers sat up. "Where?"

"The Colonial House. Do you know it?"

Withers knew. It was one of the biggest mansions in the area. "Yeah. What happened?"

There was a pause, and Withers got the distinct impression the guy on the other end was being prompted. It was just that sheriff feeling he got now and then. "You'd better get out here... now," the voice said.

"What's your name, friend?" Withers asked, trying to put a soothing touch to his words.

Another pause. "Never mind that. Get someone out here, quick."

"We're on our way. Hang in there, bud. We'll be with you in twenty minutes. But at least give me your name."

The phone line became muffled, and Withers had visions of somebody trying to get hold of the receiver. His thoughts weren't logical, but what can you do about it. The voice broke through: "Just hurry."

The line went dead, and Withers put down the phone and gathered his wits for a few seconds, before phoning a deputy. He had three, but his favourite, and the most adept, was Dawg Janowski, and Withers knew he would relish this challenge, even if it did mean leaving his wife and young son at this time of the evening.

When Janowski answered, Withers said drily, "You're not going to believe this..."

Chapter Four

Withers and Janowski were standing outside the mansion of one Leroy Figgis the Fourth. A number of police vehicles were scattered around the property and down the drive. Forensics and other technical workers had been in residence for a couple of hours now, and were coming and going, scurrying from room to room and back to their vehicles, dressed in their protective clothing. The sheriff had taken a good look at the murder scene, but his deputy had chickened out after a few minutes. He'd never come across anything like it before. Mind you, John Withers had also gone a little pale before he, too, had beat a hasty retreat.

Now they were waiting for someone. An hour ago, his boss had phoned, his speech curt and official. "John, I've had instructions from on high."

"Yes," Withers had answered, not really listening, his mind turning over the crime scene and its possibilities.

"They wanted to run this case. It's too big for us, they said." The captain's voice had dripped with anger and frustration.

"Who's they?" Withers had asked. "Special agents?"

"Leroy Figgis was a big fish, John. It's only to be expected." The captain had paused, the silence deliberately pointed. "I've made it absolutely clear that I want it left in your hands, John. I said that you'll do things by the book." There had been a faint chuckle down the line. "*Your* book, I mean!" Then he had hung up.

Withers didn't like it, but he understood. This was way too big for a hick sheriff and his hillbilly deputies – it needed the expertise of a federal agent. Bullshit, mused Withers, popping another mint in his mouth. He could handle this, no problem. And now he had the total backing of his superior.

He offered the mint packet to Janowski, who declined. Instead, the deputy shuffled the stack of glossy photographs in his hands and, despite his nausea, looked through them again.

"Not good," said Withers simply.

"No, boss," replied Janowski, studying one particular photo. "Why do you suppose they did *this* to him?"

"Well, I'm no expert," said Withers, the irony wasted on his young deputy, "but as a first thought I'd say revenge."

"Really? For what?"

"Ah," sighed Withers, "that's the question. If only we could ask the head."

Janowski wasn't impressed with the black humour, but he let it pass. "It wasn't done to the others."

"No. They were obviously lesser pawns in the game," Withers said, pleased that he had got in a reference to his favourite pastime.

Janowski again missed it. "And the woman?"

"One has to assume she was clearly in the wrong place, as they say."

They were interrupted by the arrival of a black saloon with tinted windows, which pulled up beside Withers' patrol car. They watched intently as the door opened and a man stepped out, dressed in a black suit, crisp white shirt and pencil tie, a pair of Ray Bans shielding his eyes from the glare that was so obviously prevalent at ten o'clock in the evening.

Dickhead, thought Withers rather ungallantly.

The man was thin, rather like his tie, with a pock-marked face and a bulbous nose. Think George Clooney and Schnozzle Durante. He walked with a slight limp as he approached the two officers, smiling and throwing out his hand in greeting.

"Hi, I'm Pat Rafferty. Sent to help you guys out." His voice had the slightest lilt of the Irish and his grasp was tight as he pumped their hands. "Sorry if I look a bit like a Man in Black, but I have to wear these things because my eyes react to any kind of light. Born with it, I'm afraid."

Withers mentally took back the dickhead jibe. "I'm Sheriff John Withers, and this is Deputy Dawg…"

The deputy passed yet another internal sigh. He'd been with the sheriff for two years now, his first ever posting, and still the man couldn't get his name right. He just didn't understand it. "The name's *Doug*… Doug Janowski."

Rafferty smiled. He got the reference. "Yes, I've heard all about you guys. Pleased to meet you, Doug. Is that the photoshoot?"

Dawg nodded and handed the photos over. Rafferty studied them and exhaled. "What a mess." He looked at Withers. "Can we get something straight from the outset, John? I'm here to assist you, not take over."

Yeah, thought Withers, a little bitterly. Pull the other one.

Handing the photos back to Dawg, Rafferty suggested, "Shall we go in?" and waited for John to take the lead.

"Sure," Withers responded flatly, stepping over the threshold into the hell that was the Colonial House.

It had got the name because of its style – built in the mid-twenties in the image of Groot Constantia, a Dutch house at the centre of the famous wine area in Cape Town, South Africa, by Andres de Vries, an Afrikaner diamond-trader friend of Henry Ford, who lost it in the Great Crash of 1929. Diamonds may be forever, but the dream-house bubble was over in less than five years. Andres himself lasted barely two weeks longer, plummeting from an office window when the creditors began to call. Leroy Figgis the First took over the mansion.

Withers led them through the doorway, the police guard at the door waving them on. They stopped inside, so that Rafferty could take in the first casualty, a middle-aged woman, clearly of Hispanic descent, propped against the wall, one bullet hole each in her chest and throat.

"Mrs Dolores Gonzalez," Dawg said, as if introducing two strangers to one another, or perhaps announcing the arrival at a party of one of the guests.

Rafferty eyed him. "Yes?" he encouraged.

"Housekeeper. Fifty-nine. Been with the household for ten years. Nothing else pertinent at this stage."

Withers ushered the others along the hall, Rafferty stopping at the two large paintings. "Frida Kahlo," Withers explained. "Mexican artist. Both are originals."

Rafferty raised an eyebrow. "Really? Even more impressive than I first thought, although not to my liking."

Withers tilted his head. No taste, some people, he thought. Give him either one of those marvellous paintings, and he would be in heaven forever. "What do you like, then?" he asked, expecting Rafferty to come out with some obtuse ultra-modern dabber.

"Old masters," Rafferty said with feeling. "Me, I'm into *really* old things!"

"For example?" asked Withers, a mite bewildered.

"The two Frans, actually: Holbein and Hals."

Withers had no come-back to that one.

Another officer stood guard at the door to the conference room, opening it as Withers approached. "Forensics finished?" Withers asked.

"As far as I know, sir," said the officer, giving what appeared to be the slightest of bows to his sheriff. Rafferty made a note of it: John Withers was obviously held in high regard.

He trailed in after the other man, followed by Dawg, still clutching his photographs. Rafferty stopped in his tracks, his mouth open.

The three bodies were still *in situ*, more technicians studying them as if they were some kind of scientific experiment, which in some ways they were. Two of them looked almost peaceful, death obviously coming quickly, judging by the one bullet hole in each temple.

Leroy, however, was a different matter. Some maniac had gone to town on him, thought Rafferty.

"Worse than you expected?" asked Withers, gaining a small modicum of pleasure from the agent's discomfort.

"I've seen a few, John. But this beats all the crap. What, exactly, have we got?"

Withers looked at his deputy, who selected one of the photographs and turned it over, ready to read the information he had previously written on it. The sheriff opened, "At the head of the table, if you'll excuse the pun, we have Leroy Figgis the Fourth."

Dawg said, "Yes, Leroy Figgis. Aged fifty-three, married..."

"Wife not in the house?" interrupted Rafferty.

"No, sir. She was on some trip or other. Name's Catherine..."

"Figgis," added Withers, somewhat unnecessarily.

Dawg snorted, then coughed to hide it. His boss often did this sort of thing, just to unsettle him. "Yes, boss," he agreed, with a look that might have made a lemon seem sweet.

"Good," said Withers with a grin. "Shall we get on?"

If you'll let me, Dawg almost said. "Leroy Figgis, aged fifty-three, married to Catherine, aged thirty-eight. Been together four years."

"Very nice, too," said Withers cheerfully.

"Figgis is... *was* the great-grandson of..."

"Leroy Figgis." Withers just couldn't help himself.

"Leroy Figgis the First, the man who created the Mercurial Bank." Dawg paused for effect. "Leroy – *our* Leroy – was worth an estimated ten billion. Everything presumably goes to his wife."

"That's a pretty little motive," mused Rafferty.

"But would a wife have her husband murdered like... *that*?" Dawg's lips curled with distaste.

"Unlikely, as you say, Dawg. But we know nothing about the good Mrs Figgis the Fourth. We can't even pin down a birth or marriage certificate. Now, victim number two," urged Withers, pointing to the body to the left of Leroy. He couldn't help but stare for a second at the neat hole drilled in the man's head.

Dawg chose another photo and flipped it. "Piers Fleming, aged forty-seven, single, probably gay..."

Withers and Rafferty shared a look. Rafferty voiced their thought. "Probably?"

"Can't be sure, sir. We have no record of any, er, liaisons."

Another look passed between the two older men. *Liaisons?* Neither said a word.

Dawg continued, unaware. "Victim knew Figgis through the bank. Apparently worked for him for the last four years." Withers indicated the other body. Dawg flipped another photo and said, "Nathaniel Cameron, aged forty-five, divorced fifteen years ago. No children, wife kept the dog. He also began working for the Mercurial Bank four years ago. The same day as Fleming, in fact."

"Interesting," said Rafferty, and Withers suddenly saw him as a vision of a cloaked Sherlock Holmes, puffing on his pipe and stroking his violin. But he knew what the agent meant.

"Four years," he said. "That seems to be a recurring theme in the life of Mr Leroy Figgis. His wife of four years, and two employees starting on the same day four years ago. Must be more than a coincidence."

Rafferty nodded. "Can we check that out?"

"Yes, sir," said Dawg.

"There is one other thing," said Withers drily, looking at Rafferty while pointing out the window to a silver saloon with a body slumped in the driver's seat.

Chapter Five

It was unfortunate. But it had to be done. Ty Cobden had a soft spot for young Ralphie Baxter. He was a good kid, although not the brightest tool, and he was happy to take orders. However, his recent experience had unhinged him, and he had become a liability. Ty couldn't take a chance on liabilities.

When he had moved away from the car, Baxter had thought it was to let him drive off into the sunset. He had told Ty that he was going on a very long trip – and wouldn't be back. Ty so wanted to let him be, but what could he do? He had no choice, even though his heart was a little heavy.

He had actually stepped back from the car so that when he fired, the blood would not splatter him. Obviously, he was going to incinerate all his outer clothing, but he didn't want the cops picking up even the slightest clue. He had to stay ahead to get even with the Arsehole who called himself the General.

After shooting Baxter, Ty had taken a leisurely stroll through the grounds, before taking off his protective clothing and putting it in the holdall. He even heard the police sirens as he scaled the perimeter wall. It was then just a case of strolling back to his car on Rift Street. Easy.

Now he was resting on a bed in a cheap motel in Thurlow, a nothing town just down the road from Bakerton. He'd found it by chance, cruising the area and deciding that it was far enough away that the locals wouldn't get too suspicious. He needn't have worried. The only local he met was the lanky, spotty teenager in the dirty reception area, picking his nose and flicking it as far as he could. Ty had been watching through the window, and as he walked in, the boy had given a little yelp of delight, presumably because he'd created a record with his snot-toss. He showed no embarrassment as he wiped his face with the sleeve of his shirt and grinned like a loon. "Hi. Lookin' for a room?"

Ty just said, "Yeah." A deep and meaningful conversation was clearly off the table.

"Just you?" the boy asked, reaching for his register under the counter. Ty flinched at the sudden movement, then settled.

"Just me."

"Name?"

"Martin Navratilova."

The boy looked impressed. "Foreign, eh?"

"Good spot!" Ty said, a smile not far from his lips. "Father was Czech."

"Wow!" enthused the boy. "Ain't never had no Czechs here before." He stopped, his mouth open, possibly catching one of the flies which hovered over the remains of someone's panini which had been left on the windowsill. "Where is Czech exactly?" he asked eventually, his face a mixture of utter confusion and total ignorance.

This time, Ty did smile. "A long way, son. My room?"

He was handed his key and given directions, before the boy went back into his shell, oblivious to everything around him, especially the Czech Republic.

Ty didn't like the idea of using motels, because they could be easily traced, but he had to stop somewhere for the night, and he sure as hell wasn't hanging around in Bakerton. Tomorrow he would try to rent a small place because he felt that he might be here for a while.

He didn't fully understand the geographics of where he was. On the map he had bought before his trip down, it said 'Thurlow', but the sign at the town limit proclaimed 'Thurlow Junction'. What the hell was that all about? Taking a look at the poky little place, he was tempted to go back to that sign and write 'Pop. 20' underneath. There were probably more pigs in the pen than people.

It was dark outside, but the motel sign flashed by his window, so Ty lay back and found a position in a shadow where he could rest his eyes, his mind crystal clear.

The Arsehole was alive. Say that again, man – *he's alive*. And he's killed Leroy, P and Nat, three of the guys on the trip.

The vein in Ty's neck began to throb as the old wound started to ache and a foreboding feeling crept over him. He hadn't been like it for four years, not since he was Lucas and...

****

The private jet taxied down the runway, its six occupants mostly comfortable and talkative. Piers Fleming, known to them all as P, was the liveliest, happy to be going on this latest adventure. A tall, willowy man, with almost femininely high cheekbones and a mischievous glint in his eye, he'd just split from his sometime secret boyfriend and needed action to cleanse himself. It was hard having to hide his sexual tendencies at home and work. His ageing parents in the backwoods would most certainly not have approved, and his previous boss would have fired him on the spot for even thinking about it. Thank God Leroy was more understanding. This trip was going to be the one to make P – and, not only that, but he stood to pick up a couple of million, as did the others. He sipped happily on his gin and tonic.

"Hey, Nat, gonna help me spend my ill-gotten gains?" he asked, a wide grin on his face.

Nathaniel Cameron was unsure of P, and it showed. He was the quietest of the group, a little overweight and conscious of the fact, and with a profound fear of overt homosexuality. He had never been sure if it was because he longed to try it or hated the thought with a vengeance. Either way, he was fighting it. "No thanks, I don't mix in your circles."

The others laughed, while P pretended to take offence. "What circles would that be, pretty boy?"

"Forget it."

"Aw, c'mon, man. What are my circles?"

"He must mean the ones under your eyes," said Lucas, attempting a defuse.

The one who called himself the General leant forward, putting down his Malibu and Coke on the table. He fingered the huge ring on his finger. "I'll help you out, P. You fuck 'em, and I'll spend your money!"

The youngster, Ralphie Baxter, chuckled nervously. He wasn't into chat like the others, preferring to concentrate on the matter at hand and follow instructions to the letter. The others looked at him, and he went red.

"What about you, Ralphie? You comin' into P's circle with me?" asked the General, a smirk on his face. Ralphie shrugged, hoping that would be the end of it. It wasn't. "I bet P's pals would like a young thing like you. What d'ya say, P?"

Lucas looked imploringly at Leroy, and the older man said, "Okay, guys, cut it out. Let's concentrate on what we're about to do."

There was a murmur of something not quite like dissent before they all went quiet.

Leroy cleared his throat before continuing. "This trip is a little more special than previous ones. My contact has arranged two pick-ups this time, which means we need two teams. I, of course, will lead the first, with Nat and Lucas. Ralph, I want you to take team B…"

There was a collective release of breath. "Are you sure, Mr Figgis?" asked Piers, speaking for the others.

"You have a problem with that, P?"

"No, sir, but…"

"Ralph has my full support. Remember that." Leroy glowered at the others. "Now, as I was saying, Ralph will lead, with P and the General. The most important thing is that I don't want anybody to find out that any of us are fluent in Spanish."

"These guys aren't stupid," broke in the General. "They'll expect you to have a translator."

Leroy stared him down. "Trust me on this. I have conducted several trips with Nathaniel, and we have never needed to divulge his secret. However, this time we are meeting new suppliers... ones that I do not yet have full confidence with. It will be apposite to remain wary until credentials are confirmed."

The General looked confused by Leroy's explanation, but the darkness in his eyes was clear for all to see.

Lucas took stock: the General was the new boy, and already he spelled trouble...

****

Ty got off the bed and looked through a chink in the curtain. The neon light was glinting off the wet car park from the brief downpour a couple of hours ago. There was very little movement outside, as the motel was fairly remote, and he had made sure his room was at the back, in case he needed a quick breakout. A black sedan pulled out of a bay and swung past his window, the owner oblivious to anything but the rasping tones of Springsteen on his radio.

Ty was still smarting over what had happened. Hell, what a mess. Four of them dead, one of them at his own hands. And the Arsehole on the prowl. He didn't need this. He had been fine living up on the coast, sharing his life with a trio of very attractive women, which was no mean feat for a guy in his late forties. Though he was still pretty good-looking, in a rugged, *Magnum PI* sort of a way, minus the tache and plus the scar still livid on his neck where the Arsehole had...

****

The plane touched down, and the six men climbed out into the heat of a near-tropical day.

"Hell, man," sighed Nat, "is it always this hot?"

Leroy smiled. "If we want the goods, Nat, we need to pay with sweat."

"And there's plenty of that!" exclaimed P, taking a scented lace handkerchief from his breast pocket and dabbing his forehead.

The others smiled at his eccentricity as they moved through the little airfield building and out the other side, where two very old Land Rover Defenders were waiting, engines revved.

One of the drivers gave a half-hearted salute to Leroy. "Mr Pandando is waiting, sir," he said, the 'sir' delivered with no little sarcasm.

They climbed into the Defenders, in their teams, and held on as the vehicles raced off, churning dust and insects in their wake. The drive was thankfully short, although mighty uncomfortable, and the men were happy to dismount and accept the water bottles offered to them by a boy of no more than fifteen, who P was eyeing up with a lecherous grin. He squeezed the boy's bottom as he took the water, and the boy smiled innocently – or perhaps not so innocently.

Lucas stepped between them and urged P forward. "Let's get inside, guys. This heat's a killer."

They trooped into a hut set in the middle of a compound, surrounded by forests of massive bald cypress trees, and were told to stop in front of a rickety desk, at which sat a fat little man, his bird-like nose protruding beneath a huge pair of wire-framed glasses. His narrow little eyes darted from one man to another, seemingly taking in the character and inner workings of each one.

"Mr Pandando..." began Leroy, but he was stopped by the raising of a chunky arm. He waited.

Pandando was used to giving the orders. This was his island, and let no one forget it. He hated coming into this crummy part of it, alive with mosquitoes and God knows what other parasites, but he didn't want his contacts anywhere near his home. That was his haven, his reward for having to deal with the scum of the earth – and now that included the multi-billionaire standing before him, because he had moved on from his previous deals to something far more dangerous. And that worried Pandando.

After his inspection of the men, Pandando leant back in his chair, which almost groaned under the sudden movement. He looked intently at Ralphie and the General, before locking eyes with Leroy. "I am *so* pleased to see you again, Mr Leroy. It has been too long…"

"Two years," Leroy said.

"Ah, yes, my friend. Your last visit was extremely profitable… for both of us."

Leroy nodded. "Indeed. And now you have something else for us."

Pandando sat forward, the chair sighing beneath his overflowing buttocks. "All in good time, my friend." He looked at P, who blew him a kiss, making Pandando blush. He remembered some wild times with P, but it was better that they were kept locked away. Perhaps he could open that particular trinket box later, when the work was done. He offered P the faintest of smiles, before his eyes rested on Ralphie. "I see, Mr Leroy, that you have two new recruits."

Leroy said, "You remember Nathaniel and Lucas..."

"I do."

"And Piers, of course."

Pandando blushed again. Did Leroy know something, or was it just Pandando's imagination? He had been so discreet, he thought. Or had he? He swallowed hard. "P is also an old friend, as you say. But what of these others?"

Leroy indicated Ralphie. "Ralph Baxter, known to us as Ralphie. Young, but extremely dependable."

"Very good," said Pandando, wondering how dependable this young man might really be. He was certainly worth exploring later.

"And this gentleman," continued Leroy, "goes by the title of the General."

"Really?" smiled Pandando. "Then am I to discuss matters with the General, instead of with you, Mr Leroy?"

"The General is merely a foot soldier, my friend. He knows his place," said Leroy, but Pandando recognised the glint in the General's eyes – for he, too, had that glint the day he took control here...

Pandando opened the elaborate Tunbridge-ware box on his desk – a gift from a grateful English criminal escaping extradition – and took out two beautifully crafted Cuban cigars. He always got a hard-on when he caressed one with his fingers, thinking of nubile young Cuban girls rolling the tobacco on their thighs. Pandando was a man who liked both slices of the sexual pie, preferably running concurrently. He offered a cigar to Leroy, who took it for what it was – a sign that these were the two men in control, and everybody, including the General, should be wary of crossing them.

Lucas reached forward with his lighter…

****

Ty fingered the lighter absent-mindedly, as his mind came back to the present. He placed the lighter on the bedside table and pulled the duvet over himself. He started to shiver and knew what was coming. He was sweating, and the noises were in his head again. He knew he wouldn't sleep much, but he tried to close his eyes anyway, curling himself into a ball. Despite the torment he was going to suffer tonight, he knew that only one thing mattered now. He had to find the Arsehole…

DAY TWO

Chapter Six

It was barely seven in the morning, and already the horde was gathering in the street below the sheriff's office. Withers had fended off several of the pesky reporters as he made his way into the building, but that was only the beginning. Five of the press's finest at least had the decency to phone, so his deputies could put them in their place without too much trouble. One tried to barge into his office, but a deputy put him in an armlock and frogmarched him out of the building, the air turning ultramarine as he complained of police brutality in a police state. He'd be in a salt mine by now, if that was the case, mused Withers.

The last scribe was altogether a different matter. She asked politely to see Sheriff Withers and, when told he was busy, she sat demurely in the outer office, legs crossed, notebook in hand… and waited.

She'd been there for half an hour before Deputy Lenier went in to see Withers on a police matter. "Oh, by the way, boss," he added as an afterthought, "there's another reporter outside."

Withers sniffed. "Thought I could smell something. Send him on his way, Phil."

"I don't think *she'd* go, boss," said Lenier with a smile. "Good-looking, though." He went out, closed the door and left Withers with a bemused look on his face. Lenier opened the door again and announced, "She said she'd wait, boss," and closed the door, but not before registering the look on the sheriff's face. Lenier mentally placed a bet, and he won it two minutes later when he was asked to show the lady in. Pity Doug Janowski wasn't in, otherwise I could have made a killing, thought Lenier, the grin writ large on his face.

"Yes, thank you, Phil," Withers said pointedly and waited for his deputy to leave. "Please, Miss... er..."

"Judith Wiseman, of the *Altona Oracle*."

"Right," stuttered Withers. "Please, sit down, Miss Wiseman."

As she did so, he watched her intently. She was probably in her late thirties, a shock of auburn hair framing a quite beautiful face, with high cheekbones and light brown eyes of such crystal clearness that he could see himself in both of them. He held his breath for a moment as she uncrossed and re-crossed her legs, *à la* Sharon Stone, but with far more dignity and just a fraction less sexual tension. He was sure his mouth was open, but he couldn't help himself. He just hoped he wasn't drooling.

"Are you all right, sheriff?" she asked in a very slight English accent, all the time knowing very well that he wasn't. Judith Wiseman knew the effect she had on men, and it came in handy sometimes for her job, but she was not a predator nor someone's sexual toy. She just liked to tease.

Withers adjusted his tie and sat back, using the time to regain his lost composure. "Yes, indeed, Miss Wiseman. Now, what can I do for you?"

She opened her notebook, and all at once she was the professional journalist. "You're working on the Figgis case," she started, not expecting an answer. "What can you tell me, sheriff?"

"We are preparing a press release, but you people are too quick off the mark. I'd be grateful if you'd wait until we release something."

"I'm sure," Judith purred, "but our readers are intelligent people, sheriff. They know that one of the richest men in the country has been slain in your little town, and they want answers."

"As do we all," said Withers with a flourish of his arms. He didn't know why he did that – for some reason, he just didn't feel himself.

She studied him and liked what she saw. "I interviewed Leroy Figgis last year," she announced, as if that might encourage him to open up.

"Really?" he said. "What did you make of him?"

Judith gave a little sexy laugh. "I'm disappointed, sheriff," she admonished him gently. "I thought you may have read my piece."

"I have no interest in such things, Miss Wiseman." He stopped himself, aware that he may have offended her. "I'm sorry if that sounds rude…"

"Not at all," she replied, sucking on her pencil. "But you may have got a real insight into the man, that's all."

Withers leaned forward. "So, tell me."

"Leroy Figgis was a complex man – like all men," she began, her eyes sparkling. "I have to say that I liked him. I found him warm, witty, strong. He was highly thought of by his employees and contemporaries, even the ones who might have been termed 'enemies' of his bank and the way he ran it. He was intelligent, and highly complimentary to me during our interview…"

"I'm sure he was." Withers wished he hadn't said that, but she seemed not to notice.

"It was, I believe, one of my finer moments of journalism." Judith paused, watching the sheriff's response. "And I don't understand why anyone would want to kill him."

Withers gave her a sardonic smile. "And yet somebody did, Miss Wiseman."

She turned away for a second to gather her thoughts, before once more looking him in the eye. "Perhaps," she mused, again sucking on her pencil, "perhaps we should go for a more personal angle."

Withers was watching her lips. "Would you not be going over old ground?" he asked.

Judith gave her little laugh. "Oh, sheriff, you misunderstand me." She met his gaze and smiled warmly. "Not Mr Figgis, silly. I have done him already. I meant you." She was visualising a double-page spread on 'The sheriff hunting a killer', with an in-depth interview with the man himself. She licked her lips, and Withers fell a little more under her spell. "What are your interests?" she continued. "How do you operate at work… at home? Is there a significant other…?"

The spell was broken. "I think this interview is over, Miss Wiseman. Please leave, so I can get on with my investigation." His face had turned a bright red, and Judith noted that he was fisting his hands, and sweat had formed across his brow.

Her demeanour also changed. "I am so sorry, sheriff. I obviously hit a raw nerve, and for that I offer my most sincere apologies. I just want to get some kind of story for the *Oracle* readers. I am not a sensationalist, despite what you might think. Please, let me make amends in some way. Have dinner with me tonight. No strings. Just two professionals, chewing the fat."

Withers stood. "That won't be necessary, Miss Wiseman. I understand that you are desperate for a story, but it will not be mine. Please leave now."

He watched soullessly as Judith got up and moved to the door. She hesitated, about to say something further, but, thinking better of it, she turned and went out, gently closing the door behind her. Withers fell into his chair, his mind racing. He hadn't thought deeply about Heather in a while, and actually believed he was getting over it... but now the spectre had raised itself again, and a tear fell from his eye.

Chapter Seven

The General was enjoying himself. He was reclining on a lounger with a glass of Malibu and Coke, gazing down onto the town of Bakerton from the stoep of a very pleasant little cabin in a landscaped garden at the edge of Copper Ridge.

He was especially happy because the previous owner had just recently departed, as reported to him by Number Three, who had tuned the car receiver onto the cops' own wavelength. It had initially come as somewhat of a shock to the General, because he had been given strict instructions to keep one of them alive, which is what he had done. He could only assume that Lucas had turned up and taken out Ralphie for his own protection. The General smiled at that thought, but had no sympathy at all for Ralphie Baxter.

He had whined and cried all through the affair, especially when he was instructed to cut off Leroy's hands. It was a simple enough request, and the General had made the choices pretty clear to him, so eventually Ralphie had decided that his own hands were worth more than his boss's. Not much of a choice at all, really. The General was only sorry that Leroy had refused to speak. A brave man indeed, but the gesture was ultimately futile because he would find Lucas Black… and he would destroy him, bit by bit.

He took another sip from the glass in his gloved hand. He had insisted that they wear gloves at all times, knowing that the cops would be around some time in the future to pick up prints. He had been told about Baxter's log cabin hideaway – he knew a man who knew everything – and it was the ideal base camp from which to plan the extermination of the vermin that was Lucas Black.

Number Two came out of the swing door and joined him on the stoep. The sun was high in the sky now, its rays filtering through the trees and bouncing off the glass table-top on which the General placed his glass. "Yes?" he asked, a little annoyed at the interruption to his reverie.

"Sorry, *General*," Number Two said in a strong Spanish accent, "I thought you'd like to know that the *policías* have called in an agent."

"Really?" The General's interest was raised. "Anyone we know?"

"Pat Rafferty."

"No bells are ringing. Of course, it was only to be expected. The local cops couldn't handle something this big." He rose, stretched lazily, and made his way into the cabin. It was a reasonable size, built on one level with a lounge, kitchen/diner, bathroom and two bedrooms. The General had been impressed with the decor, which was modest but well defined, the colours mellow and relaxing. The only thing that the General had taken exception to, was the massive framed photograph of some huge-titted woman, flaunting her assets for all to see. The General had immediately banished it from sight, and it now held pride of place on the wall of the second bedroom, where Number Two could drool over it to his heart's content. The nameplate on the picture said "Salome", and Number Two would spend the rest of his life looking for her if he could. He was in love.

The General retired to his room. He had wondered if Lucas knew about this place, so had assigned Number Three to keep watch, but nothing had happened overnight, and they were all beginning to relax. However, the General knew that if Lucas Black wasn't going to find him, then he would have to try something else to tempt the man out.

He began to think about *that* mission...

****

Pandando was flexible. The General knew it from the moment they met. He saw it in the eyes, in the way Pandando's fingers twitched, and how his brow sweated just that little bit when he looked at the General. It would be a simple affair to mould the malleable Pandando to the General's whim, meaning that they could have worked together to dispose of Leroy's men when the time came, and to pocket whatever loot was in the offing. If only the General hadn't been under strict instructions, he would have seriously entertained the idea of hijacking whatever they were on the island for. He knew for a fact that it was worth a tremendous amount of money, and it was a crying shame that he was to get only a small percentage of it. No, Pandando might be easily managed, but that was going to have to wait until the next trip, when the General would be his own man.

So, he sat silently, listening to the two leaders discussing the way forward.

"There are two pick-up points this time," began Pandando, "as I explained to you."

"Understood," replied Leroy. "That is why I have added to my force. I have enough men to cope."

Pandando nodded. "There should be no problems. My men will take you to the rendezvous in the morning. You will collect the parcels and be back here before sundown. You have the money?"

Leroy indicated that Lucas should place the bag he was carrying onto the table and unzip it. Inside was a laptop. "I do not deal in cash, Mr Pandando," said Leroy. "I deal only in trust and bank accounts."

Pandando smiled. "Very wise, I am sure. However, I cannot speak for my contacts. They are very simple men."

"With offshore bank accounts," said Leroy.

Pandando tilted his head sagely. "That is most certainly true, my friend." He rose, puffing on his cigar, and led them to the door. "I received your payment this afternoon, so our business is done, Mr Leroy. I will not see you in the morning, but my Number Two here will guide you and your men. *Buenos días.*"

As he left, the General studied the Number Two. He was roughly the same height, but with a more rounded figure, although it was clearly muscular. He had long black tousled hair and a wild, matching beard, both of which covered vast swathes of his face. Like all of Pandando's men, he wore combats and carried an assault rifle strapped over his back. Not the sort of person you would want to meet in a dark alley. The General was very impressed.

The six men retired to their quarters, a rough-timber outhouse some way from Pandando's office hut. It held ten bunk beds and a bathroom which barely fitted the word, having three holes in the dirt and a stench so acrid that one or two of the less well-travelled men retched every time they went near. The door to the place was falling off two very rusty hinges, and it creaked as it swung. P, the delicate flower that he was, refused to use it, preferring to conduct his ablutions under a spreading yellow mombin tree round the back of the quarters.

Thankfully, they were to stay there only the one night. In the morning, they each donned the combats supplied by Pandando. P pulled a face. "I look *dreadful!*" he moaned.

"Yes, you do," Lucas agreed, "but we still love you."

"In your dreams!" snapped P, and they all laughed, the mission forgotten in one moment of comradeship. The General stayed silent.

They climbed into the Defenders and drove into the forest. Pandando had supplied all the equipment they could possibly need, from food and drink to high-velocity rifles. He had also sent along three men, two of whom were driving, while the third sat in the back of one of the Defenders next to the General. Number Two spoke very good English, and they were soon in an animated and private conversation.

Chapter Eight

"We have an ID on the guy in the car," said Dawg, his head peeping round the corner of Sheriff Withers' office.

Withers was still at his desk and was now fully recovered from the incident with Judith Wiseman, although it had taken time. He had such conflicting feelings that for a moment it had frightened him. The journalist was truly a beauty, as well as intelligent and fun-loving. He could easily see himself falling, if it wasn't for Heather's outstretched arms holding him back. With a sigh, he beckoned his deputy in. Rafferty was standing at the window, looking down at the street. He turned as Dawg entered.

"What have we got?" Withers asked.

Dawg put a file on the desk. "Ralph Terence Baxter. Twenty-nine. Worked for Leroy..."

"Don't tell me," interrupted Withers, before Rafferty could do so, "he joined Figgis Enterprises four years ago."

Dawg nodded. "Same day as the others."

"I'll be jiggered!" said Rafferty, taking a seat opposite the sheriff.

"Is that the Irish in you coming out?" Withers asked, smiling.

"To be sure," Rafferty replied, emphasising his Irish lilt just a tad.

Dawg waited. Then, "There's something else, boss."

"Well?"

"Baxter was killed with a different gun."

"Really?" said Rafferty.

"Interesting," said Withers.

"The other three were killed by a Glock 17. The bullet that did for Baxter was fired from a Heckler VP70, reasonably close range, through the victim's left ear... and out his right," explained Dawg, dropping the file on the desk with a crash. "One bullet, and good night."

"None of this is making much sense," said Withers. "We're obviously looking for two separate killers."

"Agreed," said Rafferty. "It's pretty unlikely that the killers of Leroy Figgis would let Baxter go, only to kill him later with a different gun."

"Let's start at the beginning," suggested Withers, more talking to himself than Rafferty or Dawg. He was getting in the zone now, his mind in overdrive. "There was no sign of forced entry, so we have to assume somebody – Mrs Gonzalez, almost certainly – let them in."

Dawg was pondering. "Do you think she knew them?"

Withers nodded. "We saw nothing to suggest there had been a struggle at the entrance. My guess is that she opened the door fully knowing who was outside and that they were carrying firearms. Which begs the question: was she part of the gang?"

"But they killed her!" said Dawg with some feeling.

"Yes," agreed Withers. "But remember where her body was found. It was some way away from the door, meaning that she must have let them in and then perhaps started to head for the side door, thinking her job was done. Once the killers were in, they were then ready to start disposing of the occupants…"

"Starting with the housekeeper," joined in Rafferty.

"And using silencers on their weapons, otherwise Figgis and the others would have heard and might have had time to escape," concluded Withers.

Dawg was still not convinced. "But if she was in on it, why did they shoot her?"

"I'll pass on that one for now, Dawg," said Withers. "They left Baxter as a witness, so eventually perhaps he would have guessed that the housekeeper was involved. Possibly they were covering their tracks. Or maybe she just got greedy. We may never know, of course. But what came next" – and here Withers took a breath, fighting back the anger mounting in him – "was an act of savagery I have never seen the like of before. According to the MO, Figgis's hands were chopped off and his body mutilated before the final shot in the head, again between the eyes."

"And decapitation," Rafferty added as a very large full stop.

"Just so," murmured Withers, still brooding over the guilt or otherwise of the housekeeper.

"So, what about the guy in the car, Baxter?" asked Rafferty.

"Ah," said Withers, "this is where things become much more cloudy. We know that Baxter was seated at the table at some stage – forensics have confirmed as much – but we're not sure what role he played. And why would the killers not finish him off in the room, like the others?"

"Apart from the obvious fact he was found outside, the blood on the walls and on his body show he did make his way to the door and beyond *after* the event," Dawg joined in, now getting to grips with the case. "So, they must have let him go…"

"Any chance he escaped?" asked Rafferty, knowing the answer before he spoke.

"No," said Withers. "They let him go. No doubt about it."

"He's a material witness. Nobody in their right mind would let him leave that room alive," said Dawg.

"Unless," mused Withers, "they needed him to *act* as a witness, to tell the world what had happened." He paused. "Or to tell *someone* what had happened."

Rafferty had got the drift. "Someone out there that the killers are hunting. A message to say that they are after him, and they will stop at nothing to track him down."

"So, Baxter was in touch with this someone," said Dawg, a little confused again. When Withers nodded, he continued, "So why didn't they just get Baxter to phone this guy and get him over?"

Rafferty looked at Withers before saying, "It's likely he isn't local. He's out of town somewhere. Perhaps they sent Baxter out to go find this guy."

Dawg swirled it round in his mind. "But he was found at the back of the house…"

"Yes," said Rafferty, "that is puzzling."

Withers said, "Not at all. I think Baxter found who he was looking for and brought him back to the house. Then, this unknown quantity became our second killer."

Chapter Nine

The flat was perfect. Ty paid cash for a month's stay, hoping that would be enough time. In fact, to his mind, that was far too long. He wanted this settled now. He had spent the morning looking for a suitable base, first on the outskirts of Bakerton, then settling for this place in Thurlow Junction, actually a stone's throw from the motel he had stayed in last night. That really annoyed him. He'd wasted three hours.

The landlord now knew him as Bill Murray, and even joked that he looked like the comedy actor, even though that was blatantly untrue. Ty had smiled weakly at that, before saying goodbye and shutting the door on him. He was now in a two-room flat consisting of a bedroom with an excuse for an en-suite, and an all-inclusive living area, complete with stove and two-person dining table set, which had mismatched chairs and a crack on the plastic laminate table-top. The walls were a dirty shade of white, with the occasional palm print and stain to break up the monotony. There was a bad painting of Jesus Christ in a frame on the wall, which Ty turned over, and a framed prayer, which Ty read and digested. He might need a little help from above later.

He sat at the table and opened the sandwich he had bought. Tuna and mayo. Not his favourite, but what can you do? He chewed it without tasting, his mind elsewhere…

****

"What is the plan, *General*?" Number Two stood on the stoep and took off his gloves. He had sensitive hands and moisturised them twice a day, so the compulsory wearing of gloves was an irritant he could do without. Putting the gloves over his belt, he gently massaged each hand as he waited for a response.

The General looked at him. "Make sure you put those things back on. My prints are on record, and so might yours. We'll leave other traces, but by the time they are tested, this will be all over." He looked out over the verandah, studying the town below. He was becoming obsessed with Bakerton, and he didn't like it one bit. He realised Number Two was still waiting for an answer. At present, he didn't have one.

****

The first Defender suddenly veered to the left, throwing its occupants against the side of the vehicle. Ralphie was first to get his bearings. "We're on our own now."

The General looked out of the window as the second Land Rover ploughed on, its tyres screeching as it went over the rough terrain, and the driver was forced to brake every other second. "Mad bastard!" he said.

His own driver responded with, *"Loco bastardo!"* and the General wasn't sure if it had been a coincidence or whether the driver was translating his own outburst. He looked at Number Two, who held his gun on his lap, caressing it gently. "We are all *loco, señor,*" he said, grinning. "It goes with the job." His wide smile revealed yellowing teeth with several gaps, and the General grinned back. They were going to get on fine.

The other Land Rover was soon out of sight, and the four passengers began to relax. "We are almost there," announced Number Two. "Please be ready."

They could see rocks and swirling waves below them to the left as the Defender came to a sharp halt, again throwing them around. In front was a small, ramshackle hut, reminiscent of the old fishing shacks Ralphie had seen on his travels around the coast of his hometown, once a thriving fishing community. He watched nervously as two men emerged, each carrying pistols, and one wearing a bright red bandana over his lank, silver hair. They stood motionless as Ralphie and the others got out of the Land Rover, the General unclipping the safety catch on his rifle.

"Inside!" one of the men ordered, and nobody was going to argue.

They went through the doorway and came face to face with a Zapata lookalike, his huge moustache appearing to fill half his face. No sombrero, though, mused the General sadly. It would have made a perfect picture.

"Sit!" ordered the man who had first spoken, but Zapata waved his hand and said something in Spanish. P gave no sign of understanding, but he inwardly smiled at the name Zapata had called his subordinate.

"My apologies, gentlemen," said Zapata in a rich accent. "He is a little what you might call... over-zealous." He held out a hand in friendship, waiting for his opposite number to reciprocate.

Ralphie stepped forward and grasped his hand. "I am the representative of..."

"Mr Figgis... yes, of course. Do you have the money?"

Ralphie had been briefed just beforehand by Leroy, so knew what he was collecting. He stood upright. "I am instructed to see the goods first."

"Very wise," said Zapata, waving away one of his men. "I will show you a sample, and then you are free to inspect the shipment. However, I can assure you that it is first-grade, direct from Bogota."

"I will contact Mr Figgis," said Ralphie.

The General was beginning to understand. His boss had told him to keep a close watch on the delivery, but to do nothing to raise suspicions. But now he knew what was at stake, and how much it could be worth. He placed a cautionary hand on Ralphie's arm and whispered, "Wait. Let's see what they've got first."

The man came back with a small package and placed it on the table. "Please," said Zapata, "help yourself."

P was a regular user, so it was only natural that he should examine the white powder. Ralphie called him forward and made it clear what was required. P took his time, before saying, "Looks good, Ralphie."

Ralphie took out his mobile and began to dial Leroy's number...

Chapter Ten

The Mercurial Bank building was the biggest in the town. Even the spanking-new Mercedes showroom and office complex on Petersen Avenue looked cheapskate in comparison.

The bank building covered almost half the length of Mercurial Street – yes, the bank even named the road – and a third of Prenton Drive, which ran parallel to it. The property itself was all 'glass and brass', designed around fifteen years ago by Leroy Figgis himself and a young, up and coming architect who faded into obscurity months later. The edifice was now a silent monument to both men.

Withers had decided to go to the bank in civilian clothes – he didn't want to spook the employees too much – and, as he walked, he had enjoyed the experience, greeting one or two people he knew and basking in the late-morning sunshine. It was only when he turned into Mercurial Street that he saw them: a horde of scruffs crowded around the building and cascading out onto the street. He sucked in his breath and walked on, knowing that he would have to break through this smelly band of ne'er-do-wells and worthless human beings.

"Sheriff!" shouted someone, and Withers looked into the throng, recognising Ted Peel, local hack. "What's the latest?"

Withers brushed past him and the rest of the newspaper vultures with a "No comment". The others were all strangers, of course, plucked from every tabloid and broadsheet within a radius of two hundred miles, and probably more. He saw a Japanese face and what could have been a stern Russian, but that didn't necessarily mean worldwide exposure. Not yet, anyway. He also saw her, standing apart from the rest, pencil and notepad still in hand. She looked at him, as if begging him to stop and talk, but he had no time nor inclination to meet with Judith Wiseman, so he continued on his way.

"Aw, c'mon, John." Ted Peel was chasing after him. "Have you got any leads?"

Withers had a mental image of all these newshounds scampering around his feet, all linked to a dog lead in his hand. He grinned to himself, but outwardly looked unsmiling. "No comment." He pulled open the door to the bank and was grateful for the silent sanctuary it offered. The staff inside were in an advanced state of shock, all staring at the commotion outside and trying to digest the loss of their figurehead. A small blonde woman sat in a plush armchair in a corner, sobbing loudly, a male colleague standing beside her in an effort to soothe her, his hand draped over her shoulder, fingers perilously close to her breast. He had that look in his eye.

Withers moved over to reception and smiled at the ashen-faced young girl behind the teak-veneered desk. "I believe Mr Ross is expecting me. My deputy phoned earlier. I'm Sheriff John…"

"Yes, sir," the girl responded, ever the professional. "Top floor. The lift is over there." She pointed a beautifully manicured and painted finger. "It's a terrible thing, isn't it?"

"It is," said Withers because there was nothing else to say. He entered the lift and pressed the required button, relieved at a few moments of respite as the lift made its smooth way up to the top floor, a cultured male voice telling him which floor he was passing. As the lift hit the top floor, Withers took an extra strong and waited for the door to open.

Raymond Ross was standing in front of the lift. "Sheriff," he said, no arm extended in greeting. "About time, too." He had an English Oxbridge tone – rather reminiscent of the voice in the lift, thought Withers – but he didn't wait for a reply, smartly turning on his heels and going back into his office. Withers hesitated, then followed, by which time Ross was seated in his plush chair, swivelling slightly, with his brown Oxford brogues creating patterns in the deep-pile carpet.

"That rabble," he said, as Withers entered, "have been out there since dawn. I expect you to remove them – by force, if necessary."

"Can't do that," replied Withers, taking a seat opposite the banker.

Ross appeared surprised at the temerity of a mere pleb perching on one of his chairs without invitation. "Really? Are you not an upholder of the law?"

"I am, but they are not breaking the law," said Withers patiently.

"What about trespass… or public nuisance?"

"Sorry, Mr Ross. They are merely citizens going about their lawful business." Withers studied the other man. "I am here to talk about Mr Figgis."

Ross sat back. "Yes, of course," he said, reddening. "A nasty business."

It was only now that Withers could study the new top man at the Mercurial Bank. Thin and wiry, he looked about forty, although Withers knew that he was actually fifty-six. He had an athletic build and wore a natty, slightly-greying quiff above his chiselled and rectangular face. His brown eyes were narrow, with thin eyebrows that almost met above his over-broad nose. His lips were set slightly apart, as if ready to spit out venom to any person not toeing the line. In other words, a typical bank chairman. His smile was suddenly disarming, his voice at once smooth and irritating. "My apologies, sheriff. You will appreciate this is a very trying time for us all." When Withers nodded, he added, "So, what do you want to know?"

"Mr Figgis was the chairman…"

"*Is* the chairman," corrected Ross. "Until the board meets to appoint a new chairman, the incumbent remains in place, living or otherwise." His smile was as crooked as an occupant of one of Withers' cells. "I am senior vice-chairman, *acting* chairman."

"I understand. Thank you for your clarification, Mr Ross. Now, about Mr Figgis…"

"A fine man, sheriff. I was honoured to serve under him."

Withers somehow doubted that. "So, you can't imagine who might have wanted to cause him harm?"

Ross steepled his fingers on the desk. "In business, we make foe as well as friend, but I cannot think of anybody who might have hated him enough to do that to him."

"What, Mr Ross? What, exactly, do you think was done to him?"

Ross back-tracked. "I've heard the stories, sheriff. It was, by all accounts, pretty barbaric."

"There has been no release of any details, so these stories, as you call them, are fantasies. I suggest that you do not repeat them," said Withers, the anger strong in his voice. He waited a second before continuing, his tone more conciliatory. "Tell me about the three men who were with Mr Figgis."

"Well," said Ross quietly, subdued by the sheriff's last outburst, "Piers Fleming was the only one I actually knew. Before he came to work for the bank… er, for Leroy, he was employed by one of our clients, a translation school in the city. He spoke three languages fluently, I believe, but Leroy was more interested in his Spanish."

"Why was that, Mr Ross?"

"I have no idea, sheriff. All I know is that, once the three of them became employees of the bank, I never saw them."

"Was that not unusual?"

"Yes, but Leroy was adamant that the men be on the payroll. I naturally assumed that he was planning some kind of approach to a Spanish bank, or something," Ross finished limply.

"If it was bank business, surely you and the other board members would have been privy to what was going on?" asked Withers, confused even more.

"One would have thought so, yes. But Leroy was the chairman."

"And you were his inferior," said Withers, deliberately.

"His subordinate, sheriff; certainly not his inferior," responded Ross, his cheeks flushed.

"Forgive me, Mr Ross, I chose the wrong word," said Withers, not sounding at all apologetic.

Ross added, "It is strange that in the four years they were with us, until their deaths, none of them spent one minute at the bank. As far as I know, they always met at the Colonial House; although, of course, I cannot confirm that."

"An interesting thought. Could I possibly call upon your secretary to furnish me with details of the victims?"

Ross waved his arms. "I would love to help on the matter, sheriff, but I am afraid we have nothing at all on these individuals. For some reason, there are no records."

"Really?" said Withers, incredulous. "This is an international bank, Mr Ross. There are regulations."

"Even so, sheriff, there is nothing I can do to help you. Now, if you don't mind…"

Withers had been dismissed, and there was nothing he could do about it.

The two men stood face to face for what seemed a lifetime, before Withers made his way out of the office and back to the lift without offering a handshake. As far as Withers was concerned, you don't offer your hand to a rattlesnake.

Before reaching the lift, Withers had an idea. He quickly retraced his steps and found his way into the office of Ross's secretary. "Hi," he said, all silk and smooth.

"Hello," the woman replied. "Can I be of assistance?"

"Oh, I *do* hope so," he said, gushing. "I'd like some details about one of your employees."

"That's not possible, I'm afraid. Secrecy laws, you understand."

"Oh, I do, I do. It's just that this is a little... personal. How can I put this? Piers was a very close friend..."

"Piers? You mean the gentleman who was killed? Oh, my, he was a friend of yours. I'm so sorry." And she meant it, too. "What did you want to know?"

"Well, his parents have asked me to present a eulogy..."

The girl smiled through her discomfort. "I see. Well, I can't really help you with any details, because I've only been here a year. I can give you the address of Mr Figgis's last secretary, if that would help."

Withers gushed anew. "Oh, that would be so kind of you. Thank you so much." He almost skipped out of the office, still in character.

Raymond Ross looked out of the window at the mass of reporters below and sucked air through his teeth.

The General had gone too far…

****

Leroy answered the phone, listened, nodded and said, "Thank you, Ralphie. Lucas will send the money over now."

Lucas laid the laptop on a desk and typed in the password. A baffling array of figures came up on the screen, enough to confuse the smartest of mathematicians. In fact, it was a unique program Leroy had got some computer expert to create which hid the movement of assets between Leroy's private accounts and any other global account he chose to access. Lucas had been instructed on its use, and now he tapped in a code which changed the screen to show just three columns of numbers. He clicked the mouse on the top row of the first column to highlight it, then dragged it to the top of the third column, pressed return, and a mini explosion occurred on the screen, with fireworks going off and loud brass-band music playing.

"Just my little joke," explained Leroy on the telephone to Ralphie, who could obviously hear the cacophony but without the visuals. "I do like a fanfare when I play with money. Tell your supplier that the funds have been transferred, and the transaction is therefore concluded."

Eight miles away, Ralphie put down the phone and looked at Zapata. "Mr Leroy has wired over the money," he said, waiting for a response.

Zapata nodded and looked at his laptop for confirmation. He grinned, his chipped teeth shining like some old bone relics dug out of a peat marsh. Ralphie noticed several with diamond fillings and a gold-plated one left of centre and shuddered. He didn't like the image now ingrained in his mind. Zapata rose. "We are done," he said with a flourish of his hand, ordering everybody outside.

They made their way to an old Dodge pick-up which was carrying a number of large parcels, each one marked with 'Farm Fertiliser' in stencilled paint along its length. Zapata's men hurriedly lifted them down and took them to the Defender, where the driver stood, overseeing the transfer. He saw the last parcel into place and slammed down the rear door, locking it and moving back to his seat. He waited for the others to take their places.

Ralphie was extremely nervous. Anything could still go wrong; after all, he didn't have a clue who these people were, and now they had their money, they could snatch back the goods and leave him and the others in a pool of blood. Who would know? Then, his phone rang.

"Ralphie, it's Leroy."

"Yes, sir?"

"Everything in place?"

"Yes, sir."

"Good. Hand the phone to your contact." Ralphie offered the phone to a surprised Zapata, who took it and held it to his ear. Leroy's voice was severe. "Listen. My other men are watching you as we speak. If you attempt to stop the Land Rover leaving, I will instruct them to open fire. Do you understand?"

Zapata, confused and stunned at this turn of events, nodded dumbly, causing Leroy to repeat the question. "*Si,*" he finally replied, "I hear you. My men will not stop the Land Rover." In fact, the thought had never even entered his tiny mind.

"Good," said Leroy. "We will no doubt do business again." Then he hung up, and Zapata returned the phone to Ralphie, not believing for one minute that Leroy's men were in the surrounding forest, but just not sure enough to consider the possibility of reneging on the deal.

Zapata waved the Defender away and melted into the forest with his men... and his money.

Ralphie stared after him, wondering what all that was about.

It was a bluff, of course, but Leroy was confident that the local mafioso leader wouldn't have the intelligence to check it out. He'd been paid, so why would he think of taking further risks by incurring the wrath of someone as prominent and wealthy as the owner of an international bank? It would make no sense.

Leroy returned to his own dealings. He was sitting opposite a tough little man with deep-sunken eyes and a high forehead, bald as a coot and a nasty scar running across his left cheek. An altogether unsavoury character, but it had to be done.

"You have finished your other business, *señor*?" he asked sarcastically, annoyed at being kept waiting.

Leroy bowed his head. "My apologies, Mr Fidel. I am but a juggler, handling projects in both hands and also in the air."

Fidel did not understand a word. "My money, *señor* – that is all I am interested in."

"But of course." Leroy indicated that Lucas should again turn to the laptop, and this time he clicked on the second line of the first column and dragged it to the first line of the second column, pressing return and causing the fireworks to ignite.

Fidel was not at all impressed. "It is done?" he demanded, nodding to another man, who checked on his laptop. He grunted an affirmative, and Fidel relaxed. "Very good, *señor* – our business is complete. Take the packages and be gone."

Lucas put the laptop in its case and followed Leroy and Nat out of the small hut, enjoying the smell of the fresh air and knowing it was all nearly finished and he would soon get his money. He kept the finger of his right hand on the trigger of his rifle, alert for any double-cross, but it was all going smoothly. They oversaw the loading of the packages, climbed into the Defender and drove away, ready to meet the other vehicle. All was well...

Chapter Eleven

Judith Wiseman was waiting outside the bank. Not only that, but she was blocking his path. He tried to sidestep her, but she moved with him, even when he attempted to go the opposite way. He stopped. Waited. So did she. It was an impasse.

"I don't have time for this," Withers said, annoyed.

"Then let me apologise properly."

"I thought you had done so already."

"But you didn't accept it."

There was some logic in that. "No," agreed Withers, "perhaps not. But now I do."

"Ha!" Judith laughed. "I don't believe you."

"That is your choice," said Withers, once more attempting to bypass her. This time she let him go.

"One small step for a man," she said.

He stopped. "I'm sorry?"

"One small step, sheriff," she beamed. "You are at least talking to me again." With that, she melted into the crowd of reporters gathered around one of the bank staff trying to get into the building, their questions reverberating down the road as Withers finally turned away from her and started to walk back to his office.

****

Rafferty was passing a few idle minutes, but jumped out of the sheriff's chair as Withers stormed in.

"Bloody woman!" he bellowed.

Rafferty took a step back. "Aren't they all?"

"What?" Withers hadn't even noticed him. Now he just stared. "Sorry, Pat, what did you say?"

Rafferty smiled. "I was just agreeing with you, that's all."

Withers sank into his chair and absent-mindedly shuffled some papers. "Whatever."

Rafferty was ready to take the bull by the horns. "Who are we talking about here?"

"What?"

"This 'bloody woman' who seems to have got under your skin."

"It's nothing."

"Ah," said Rafferty, "but it *isn't* nothing, John. It's very definitely something."

"Leave it, Pat. Case closed."

"You know I'll winkle it out of you eventually."

Withers grimaced. "Let's concentrate on business, shall we?"

Rafferty shrugged. He would pursue the subject later.

"Sit down, Pat," urged Withers, his voice sharp. "You make me nervous hovering over me like that."

Rafferty pulled up a chair. "OK, I'm sitting comfortably."

Withers gathered his thoughts. "I've just met the new chairman – sorry, acting chairman – at the Mercurial…"

"And?"

"I didn't like him."

"Explain."

"I just didn't like him. Do I need a reason?"

Rafferty held up a hand. "Whoa, I've got a feeling that 'bloody woman' is still running around that head of yours. Now, take it easy and talk me through the bank meeting."

"Sorry. Yes, okay. This guy, Raymond Ross, showed no emotion at the passing of his colleague. I saw nothing to indicate that he gave a damn. He's just waiting to take over. But he did tell me something of interest." He paused. "He said that none of the deceased ever went to the bank. All meetings were conducted at Figgis's house."

"Strange," mused Rafferty.

"Perhaps not," countered Withers. "What if they were planning something other than bank business?"

"Then why put them on the payroll?" asked Rafferty. "If they weren't on bank business, why should the bank pay them?"

"To make it look legitimate, is my guess. To keep prying eyes out. Leroy Figgis and his cronies were up to no good." He looked at the pictures of the victims that Dawg had pinned to the wall: Leroy in life, taken a month ago at some high-brow function in the city; the others in death, their wounds carefully pixellated out to avoid undue stress to a casual observer. "According to the records, they all worked for Figgis until their deaths, although not one of them set foot in the bank. Why did Figgis get this group together, and what brought them all to this sorry end?"

****

Lunch had been taken at a rush, a sandwich devoured in a stop-start motion, like a badly created cartoon. No wonder he suffered from indigestion and rampant heartburn. He really should slow down. He rushed down the corridor, to-go coffee in hand, and almost crashed through the door to his clinic, expecting to see Mrs Milford, whose appointment had been at 1am, five minutes ago. But it wasn't her.

"Hello, doc," said Withers, sitting in the waiting-room chair, an unopened copy of *Amateur Gardening* on his lap.

Doctor Oliver Clarke stopped in his tracks. "John? What are you doing here? You should be Mrs Milford."

Withers laughed. "Hey, doc, I know you're a psychologist, but turning me into a woman won't help!"

Oliver floundered. "Sorry, John. You know what I mean. This is Mrs Milford's time."

"You mean the little old lady with the blue rinse? Oh, she got fed up with waiting. I told her you'd give her a free session to make up for it."

"Thanks," sighed Oliver, "you're so kind."

"Aren't I?"

"I just hope she survives until next time," said Oliver, only half-joking.

"She will, doc. I gave her one of my pep talks. She left here floating on air." Withers chuckled. "I'm cheaper, too!"

Oliver winced, went into his inner office and held the door for Withers. Both men sat either side of the white desk. In fact, everything in the room was white. It always reminded Withers of the inside of a morgue, which presumably was not the aura that Oliver Clarke was attempting to generate.

Oliver looked at the other man intently. "Are you okay, John?"

"What, oh, yes, I'm fine."

"It's just that your appointment is…"

Withers leant forward. "Next week, yes. I know. But I'm okay."

"Good." Oliver waited. Nothing was forthcoming. "Is it Heather again?"

Withers gave an involuntary start. "No. No, not this time."

Oliver waited. Withers took his time. "Well, it is… and it isn't."

"Okay."

"There might be someone else."

"That's good, isn't it?"

Withers wasn't so sure. "It's difficult."

Oliver picked up his expensive fountain pen and began to play with it. It became almost mesmerising for Withers. "In what way, John?"

"You know."

"Tell me."

"I love Heather…"

"Present tense?" asked Oliver, so gently that Withers could not possibly take offence.

"Yes, I think so."

"And this other woman?"

Withers chose his words. "Early days, doc."

"And you think there might be a problem about that?"

"Don't you?"

Oliver put down his pen. "What would Heather think about it?"

Although she was no longer there, Withers had often asked Heather's advice, like when he became a cop and when he was offered the position as sheriff of Bakerton. He knew she had always been behind him. But this was different. This was a takeover. "What, some other woman muscling in on her man? I don't think she'd go for that, do you, doc?"

Oliver smiled. "I get your point, John. But wouldn't she want you to be happy? Truly happy."

"I guess."

"So, what's the answer?"

"I'm paying you, doc – you tell me!"

"That's the whole point, John," said Oliver. "I can't tell you anything. You have to tell yourself."

Withers looked round the room. Nothing to see, of course, but it gave him thinking time. His eyes came to rest on Oliver's desk, and a pile of folders. He thought of his own folders, and his focus changed. "Tell me, doc, why would someone kill three people, but only mutilate one of them?"

Oliver sat upright, shocked at the question. "What?"

Withers waved an arm. "Sorry, change of subject. It's a case I'm working on."

Oliver was too professional to try to steer him back onto the original discussion. "Well, there might be many reasons. The killer may have particularly hated the one he mutilated more than the others."

"That's possible," agreed Withers, now in a safe place. As long as he didn't have to think about Heather, he could cope. "But I'm not convinced that's the answer."

"Fine. So, was the killer interrupted before he could do the same to the others?"

Withers shook his head. "No. He'd finished what he wanted to do."

"Okay. Did he torture the victim to gain information?"

"Possibly, at first," said Withers. "But surely he would have tortured the others for information as well?"

Oliver had to agree. "Yes, that is quite likely. Unless, of course, only one of them had the knowledge he was after."

Withers hesitated. "The killer did mutilate the leader of the group, which would be in line with that theory… but by all accounts, the group worked as a tight team, so the chances are they would all have the same level of knowledge."

"So, we're back to a personal attack."

"Yes, doc. I think this was pure sadism."

"Right. But what about revenge? That can be a very strong motive."

Withers was enjoying himself now. "Revenge does look likely. What are the odds on that, doc?"

Oliver picked up his pen again and twiddled. "Well, most sadists tend to concentrate on one victim. If there are more than one, then they are usually treated in the same way. If these kinds of perpetrators get the taste of blood, they will carry on until they are sated. If revenge is at work in your case, I am surprised only one victim was sadistically targeted. It goes against the norm."

"So, we're talking about two kinds of murders here?" said Withers, needing clarification.

"Obviously I don't know any of the details, John. But it could be that your killer murdered two people for one reason – and the other one for an entirely different reason."

****

Rafferty sat in his car, the tinted screen helping to shade his eyes. He had been there for over an hour, and his backside was beginning to ache. He adjusted his position several times, and even thought of getting out for a walk to stretch his throbbing leg. He wasn't cut out for this kind of work any more. It was almost time to call it a day.

As he swivelled one more time in the seat, he saw Withers emerge from the office block and sank back into the seat, even though he was invisible to anyone on the street. He watched as Withers got into his car and drove away, before taking out his phone and making a call.

"He's just been to see his shrink, but he looks fine."

The female voice on the other end said, "Keep an eye on him, Pat. We've bowed to the police authorities to give him his head, but he does have a reputation for being a loose cannon."

"Yes, ma'am," said Rafferty, throwing the phone on the passenger seat and driving after Withers.

****

The hotel room was... adequate. Pale green-painted walls, enhanced with a frieze of dark green and yellow squiggles expertly placed halfway between the ceiling and faux wooden floorboards, acted as a fitting backdrop to the single bed, itself covered in a dark green sheet and a duvet of yellow-coloured flowers. A bedside cabinet of cheap wood veneer was placed one side of the bed, while on the other side was a shelf, situated just under the frieze and acting as the resting place for a vase of yellow roses, each one beginning to wilt from the central heating which was, as is usual in hotels, set at its highest level.

A thirty-two-inch TV screen was attached to the wall opposite the bed, and below that was a desk and chair, made of the same cheap wood as the cabinet, presumably a job-lot from the Furniture Warehouse for Skinflints up in the city.

Judith Wiseman sat at the desk, a coffee beside her and her laptop open. The remains of a take-away sandwich hovered over the edge of the desk, just above a waste-paper basket, which was likely to be the sandwich's last resting place. She raised the coffee cup, almost in salute, as she pressed Send, and her latest article on the Figgis saga was flying through the ether, or whatever it flies through these days, destined for the spike at the *Oracle* office. Another masterpiece chiselled out of the English alphabet. Move over, Dalí! She took a mouthful of the coffee and stared at the now-blank screen.

Thoughts of the sheriff began to invade her space. She checked him out on Facebook, but he wasn't registered. The same for Instagram and Twitter. Wikipedia gave her ten John Withers. One was a sixty-five-year-old retired dentist who enjoyed golf and butterfly collecting. No, definitely not her

John. Although the butterflies might be quite interesting...

The next one was a mere boy of twenty-three, all-round athlete and a Blue at Oxford for rugby. She checked them all out, but none came up to scratch – not even the policeman, who, it turned out, worked as a detective in a city four hundred miles away. Close, but not close enough.

She sighed and took in more caffeine. Was she becoming obsessed with Sheriff Withers? It would appear so, she told herself without rancour. As if accepting the fact gracefully, she picked up her phone, tapped it thoughtfully against her chin a couple of times, then decided to dive right in.

"Bakerton police. How may I help you?"

Judith hesitated. "Um..."

"Hello," said Phil Lenier, "what can I do for you?"

"It's Judith Wiseman," she blurted, her face blushing a wonderful pink, all flustered and juvenile.

"Hi," Lenier responded brightly.

"Um, would it be possible to...?"

She couldn't quite finish the sentence, and there was an awkward silence, before Lenier finally said, "You wanted to speak with the sheriff? I'm sorry, Miss Wiseman, but he isn't..."

"Oh, that's okay. It's fine! No problem. I understand he's busy. Please give him my regards." And she tossed her phone onto the bed as she cringed, knowing full well that Deputy Lenier would have the widest grin on his face. How embarrassing…

Come on, girl, she told herself, let's get professional. It was clear that John Withers did not want to speak to her. She had tried, and that was an end to the matter. It was time to get back to the racy world of journalism. What next for this roving reporter? She'd done Leroy Figgis; John Withers – him again! – had refused to co-operate; so, who could she turn to? Logically, there was only one man. The new bank chairman, Raymond Ross.

****

The view of the garden from the large window would have pleased Heather. That was one of the reasons Withers had bought this place. She had been fascinated by flowers and delighted in the complexity of colour of the pansies and the scent of lilies and jasmine especially, filling the house with amazing colours and beautiful fragrances that even a man like Withers could appreciate. He looked at the vase of lilies on the table and smiled. He was no gardener, so he was thankful for Pete, his retired neighbour, coming round a couple of days a week to tend the plot. She had never seen this garden, of course, but he felt it helped to keep Heather's memory alive.

Reluctantly, he pushed away his supper plate, the food only half-eaten, as usual, and opened a second bottle of beer, enjoying the feeling as the cool liquid filled his throat. He tried to relax, but knew it was impossible. He picked up the file on the table and looked at the cover. Was he in the right frame of mind to plough through page after page? He thought not, but opened it anyway. He was still struggling to assimilate the facts as they stood. Figgis had employed three men on the same day, presumably for some reason not bank-related. They worked with him for four years and were then murdered. It made no sense. Then Withers recalled his discussion with Dr Clarke. Heather again flitted through his mind, before he thought of the savage death of Figgis himself. Could it be that he was killed for an entirely separate reason? And if so, why?

The paperwork started to become fuzzy, and he wiped his eyes. It had been a long day, and tomorrow would be more of the same. As he pushed back his chair and thought seriously about bed, she came into his head. But this time it wasn't Heather…

DAY THREE

Chapter Twelve

Grace Templeman was older than Withers had expected, probably in her late sixties, he guessed, as she stood at her door while he stepped out of his car and approached her. He hadn't mentioned anything about her to Rafferty and felt just a little guilty about that. Well, it can't be helped now. And, in his defence, Withers told himself that, after all, this is his case.

"Thank you for being so prompt," she said, leading him into her lounge. He shut the door behind him. "You would be amazed at how many workmen do not arrive when they say they will."

Withers let the reference to him being a workman pass, and sat where she had indicated he should sit, like a dutiful dog, he realised with a little wistful smile. "I got your details from the bank. Thank you for seeing me," he said.

She nodded almost royally. "If I can help in any way, sheriff, then I am pleased to do so. Mr Figgis was a fine man." She brushed her hands down her pleated skirt in a moment of contemplation. "Would you like a cup of tea?"

He hadn't expected the question. "That would be great, Miss Templeman. Thank you."

After a few minutes, she returned carrying a tray holding two Royal Doulton teacups, on saucers, and a matching teapot and milk jug. "I do not have sugar in the house, I'm afraid…"

"No problem," he lied. "I'm cutting down."

She poured his tea and took the armchair opposite, with her own cup held daintily between two fingers, the saucer resting carefully on her lap. She sipped quietly, looking intently at the sheriff. "It is a terrible thing…"

Withers nodded. "I'm sorry to be bothering you at this time. I know you were very fond of Mr Figgis, Miss Templeman."

"Please, call me Grace. It is so much easier."

Withers had to agree. "Grace, I understand you spent almost thirty years at Mercurial Bank." He had done his homework.

"That is correct."

"The last ten as Mr Figgis's PA."

"Until I retired last year, yes."

"Can you tell me about him?"

She took another sip and eyed Withers over her cup. "In what way, sheriff?"

"A good boss?"

"Extremely." She hesitated, concerned that she might say too much, but so wanting to paint a perfect picture of her former employer, especially now that he had suffered such a sad end. "In fact, Mr Figgis gave me this house on my retirement."

Withers whistled an in-breath. "Did he now? That was very generous of him."

"I told you, sheriff – he was a good man." She felt that she needed to explain a little further, just in case the policeman got the wrong impression of her. "Of course, I declined the gift." Withers nodded, as if that was what she was expecting. "He announced it at my retirement party – arranged by Mr Figgis himself, I might add – and it was very difficult to say no."

"But you did," said Withers.

"Naturally, sheriff. What do you take me for?" He shrugged an apology. "Mr Figgis said that he had bought the deeds in my name, and that I had no choice in the matter. He said it was for my long-standing support and service. I was humbled, I have to say." She almost wiped away a tear at the thought. "I finally accepted graciously – and here I am."

"And a very nice house it is," Withers said with as much feeling as he could muster. "I am sure that Mr Figgis was a good man, but do you know if he had any enemies?"

"What, enough to kill him, you mean?" Grace looked almost outraged. "I think not, sheriff. I have told you…"

"Yes," said Withers defensively, "I understand. But the fact remains that someone *did* kill him." In a horrific manner, he decided not to add, to save her sensibilities. If she only knew the full story…

"I appreciate what you are saying, sheriff, but I can think of no one so wicked. I know that Mr Ross at the bank was not a friend, but even he wouldn't…" Grace left the thought there. Withers picked it up and stored it. As Jane Austen might have written, it is a truth universally acknowledged that what is left unsaid is of equal importance to what *is* said. Grace Templeman, like Withers himself, appeared to be a very good judge of character. After a few moments of silence, he decided to change tack. "Piers Fleming, Ralph Baxter and Nathaniel Cameron…"

"What about them?" She had finished her tea and placed the cup carefully on the trolley, before reaching out to take the cup from Withers. He hadn't enjoyed it much, and there was some left in the cup. He almost shrank as he saw her disdainful look. Fortunately, she passed no comment.

"They started with the bank on the same day," he continued, slightly warily.

"They did." She looked confused at the way the conversation was going.

Withers said, "Did you get to know them?"

"A little. They always met at Mr Figgis's home and, as his PA, I attended one or two of the early meetings, although there was very little work carried out on those occasions; they were more like social events. But, apart from that, they kept themselves to themselves, as befits a senior executive."

"How senior?"

"Oh, very. Mr Figgis was adamant that the gentlemen should be considered as board level, although, of course, they were not. On the board, I mean."

"What were they like?" Withers asked.

"Well, I only really got to know one of them... Mr Fleming..."

"Piers."

"Yes, although Mr Figgis often referred to him as 'P'. A little common, I thought..."

You would, mused Withers, uncharitably, and immediately regretted it. Despite her quaint ways, Grace Templeman was a strong woman who had survived thirty years in the manly world of international banking. Some achievement.

She was still talking. "Piers had been a regular visitor to the bank for some time before he joined us, I assume as a client. I was not privy to everything, you understand. He was a very friendly, one might say avuncular, man, although a little too... *effeminate* on occasion."

Withers noted the disdain with which she said the word. "Effeminate?"

"I believe, today, he would be classified as 'gay', sheriff." She paused, as if gargling her mouth clean. "It was no concern of mine, naturally."

"What was his relationship with Mr Figgis?"

Grace looked askance. "I don't know what you are implying, sheriff, but Mr Figgis is... *was* happily married."

Withers retreated from the onslaught, blinking like prey at an oncoming predator. "Forgive me, Miss Templeman. I was referring to their business relationship."

Grace had moved up to the edge of her chair, almost as if she was ready to pounce. Her features softened as she sat back. "I see. I must apologise for my attack of truculence. It is not at all like me."

"It is understandable, considering how fond of him you were." Withers paused. "I was just wondering how the four men interacted."

Grace thought for a second. "I am not sure they did interact in any way, sheriff. Mr Figgis was clearly their superior in all respects, and I do not believe the other three were what you would call close friends. More like colleagues, really. At first, anyway..."

Withers picked up on the last three words. "At first?"

"Yes. Everyone was very business-like for the first month, but then it changed when they came back..."

He was fully alert now, sensing a minor breakthrough. He didn't like to keep repeating her words, but he still did so. "Came back?"

"From their trip. From then on, there was an atmosphere of... I don't know... *synergy*, I believe might be the current 'trendy' word."

"Synergy?" There, he'd done it again.

"It might have been my imagination," she said – although Withers doubted that very much – "but they seemed closer to each other, and at the same time... *troubled*. They..."

"Excuse me," interrupted Withers, thinking at the time that he might be taking his life in his hands, "but can we please back up a little?" He ignored her frosty stare. "They went on a trip?"

"I've told you that already."

"Yes, but to where?"

She was really looking exasperated now. "Abroad."

Withers persevered. "Where, exactly?"

Grace stood suddenly, and he was expecting her to handbag him where he sat – or perhaps give him six of the best for being a very silly boy. Instead, she left the room with a stern, "Wait," and he actually gulped. Being sheriff wasn't all it was cracked up to be, especially when you have to deal with people like Grace Templeman.

She came back barely two minutes later, clutching a red book to her ample bosom. She sat and placed the book on her lap. "This," she said, flicking through the book, "is Mr Figgis's diary of four years ago."

"You have a diary?"

"I have all of his personal diaries, from ten years ago when I became his PA until the day I retired. I also kept bank diaries in my office. Mr Figgis was very impressed with my diary recording, if I may say so." She found the relevant page. "Now, the three gentlemen joined the company on the first day of March." She ran her hand down the page, then turned over a few pages, her thumb coming to a halt around halfway down. "Yes, here we are. Mr Figgis had an appointment with a Mr Vincent Pandando, and took his private jet to Lanscarges... on the fifteenth of April."

"The island?"

"Yes, the island of Lanscarges. Mr Figgis has valuable contacts on the island. He made a number of visits there in the year before the one in question."

"Was this trip logged in the office diary?"

Grace did not have to think about that one. "The trip was business, but not bank business. So, the answer to your question would be no."

"What sort of business?"

"That was never discussed in my presence, sheriff."

"You mentioned a Vincent Pandando," said Withers.

"I did. He is a businessman on the island. I believe Mr Figgis had been dealing with Mr Pandando for several years."

"But you don't know what business." It was a statement rather than a question.

Grace arched her eyebrows. "I have already said…"

Withers withered. "Yes, sorry. My turn to apologise."

Grace nodded graciously. "Shall we continue, sheriff, now that we are even?"

Withers took a breath. "You said that the others went with him this time?"

"On the last trip, yes, I believe so."

Withers had been amazed at Grace's clerical dexterity up to that moment but was disappointed with the end result. "You believe so?" He was beginning to sound like a bloody echo.

"Paul Cassidy will know."

"Excuse me?"

"Mr Figgis's pilot. He lives in the city now, close to the airport there. Would you like his details?"

Withers was already rising. "I would be most grateful."

Grace took a cell phone from a shelf under the coffee table, flipped it open and scrolled down like a true professional. Withers marvelled at the incongruous sight of this elderly woman dextrously handling a smartphone, and then he wrote down the address in his notebook.

"We still keep in touch. He works for one of the commercial airlines these days," said Grace, as she closed her phone. "He left Mr Figgis four years ago."

Chapter Thirteen

The girl looked good. The General watched as she served a large group of reporters in the corner of the diner, taking out her little pad and licking the tip of her pencil almost provocatively. She was animated, bubbly, everything he would have liked in a mate, in a different life…

He suddenly thought of his mother. She had wanted a daughter. He could not be sure whether she wanted him as well, or just a baby girl to cuddle. All he knew was that she welcomed him into her bed from an early age, preferring to hold him rather than her husband, who always turned his back on the both of them. It was when he was a teenager that her attitude changed. She insisted he continued to share the bed with her, as usual, but she would also relieve him of his sexual tensions by using her hand on him. He was both shocked and immensely happy – and felt utterly confused. But one night she tried to climb on him, and he hit out in disgust, punching and scratching her until his father intervened. The most frightening thing was that his father blamed him and set about the boy with the belt pulled from his jeans. Naked and bewildered, the boy did what any kid would do... he reached into the bedside cabinet drawer, drew out his father's revolver, and shot him between the eyes. Ten years inside followed... and they sure changed him.

These are not excuses; they are the facts of life. But they did not turn the General into a killer. He did that all on his own.

The waitress had eased up to the General's table. "Hi."

He smiled at her. "Hi."

"What'll it be?" she asked, her tongue just protruding from those rich lips. She was sending out friendly vibes; he was receiving come-on vibes, and he wasn't sure what to make of it. He looked at her hand, seeing his mother's, imagining it touching him...

"So, are you ready to order?"

"What? Oh, yeah, sorry." He looked at the menu to hide his confusion. When he looked back at her, his eyes settled on her left breast, and he read her name badge. "Right, Millie," he said, regaining his composure, "I'll just have a bacon roll and coffee, thanks."

She put away her pad and stuck her pencil behind a curl of blonde hair over her ear. "Coming right up, sir," she said, turning so that he could watch her walk away, confusion again rolling through his mind. Too young, he thought, but old enough.

He was still enjoying happy feelings when the door opened, and a customer walked in. He was big, muscular, and he wore a sheriff's uniform and badge. He waved at Millie, said something the General couldn't hear, then sat at a table by the window.

The General knew this was John Withers, and he studied him intently. If things went badly, the chances were that this sheriff would be cuffing him; or, worst-case scenario, zipping him up in a body bag.

The General watched as the group of reporters stormed around the sheriff's table, bombarding him with questions and jostling for position. The sheriff said something, raised an arm and they parted, scurrying back to their tables, tails between their legs. Sheriff Withers had some power, thought the General with not a little envy.

"Your coffee, sir," Millie said, making him jump. "Your roll will be along shortly."

"Thanks," he mumbled, still watching the sheriff.

Millie went over to the lawman and put her arm around his shoulder, bending down so he could place a peck on her cheek. They both laughed.

That's when the General formed his next plan.

Chapter Fourteen

He should, by rights, be talking to Rafferty, at least telling him what was going on. But Withers was his own man. He had talked with Grace Templeman without Rafferty breathing down his neck, and now he was going to see Paul Cassidy, the private pilot who was no longer private. Again, mused Withers as he drove, it's that four years. What the hell is going on here?

He'd enjoyed his coffee and chat with Millie, talking about her dad and how they should all get together, but now he had to focus.

He couldn't remember the last time he'd been to Altona, reputably the smallest and most beautiful city in the country. It had wide, tree-lined avenues and boulevards to die for, with roses and bougainvillea vying for attention in all their colourful splendour. The houses, in the main, were white-painted, with elaborate wood fascias and verandahs overlooking small but well-maintained front gardens. The business premises, too, were of a high standard, many of them, like the houses, built over a hundred years ago, when Altona had been classed as a new town, nestling comfortably in the heart of God's own country.

As he steered his car around the outskirts of the city, Withers saw the extent of recent development, with new houses and partially built properties extending deep into the countryside. These were brick-built and far less appealing than those within the city-centre limits, and he thought that the council may have made a terrible error, because casual drivers might very well loop around the city, thinking that the place was an unattractive prospect. How wrong they would be.

Withers had his driver's window down, soaking in the mid-afternoon sun and the soft breeze he could feel across his face. His favourite Django track was playing.

His GPS, in a very sexy female voice, told him to take the next left, and he obeyed as if submitting to some kind of dominatrix. He wondered who she was, this bodyless woman. He suspected she was probably a middle-aged mother of four, with corns on her feet and a bum like Kim Kardashian's, but with wrinkles. The bubble was well and truly burst, so he channelled his thoughts back to Django and Leroy Figgis, jumping between the two, drumming the steering wheel as a personal accompaniment to the music.

Dominatrix breathlessly urged him to turn right, so he slipped a gear and drove smoothly into Fairlawn Avenue. "Your destination is two hundred yards ahead," she added, her job done.

Withers glided to a stop outside a neat little bungalow, built in the popular 'L' shape, with a huge bay window at the front and a crazy stone pavement meandering through a beautifully clipped lawn to the front door. Withers was jealous. He climbed out of the car, attempted to smooth his shirt and jeans from the crumpled state they were usually in, and walked to the door. He rang the bell.

Deputy Dawg had telephoned ahead, claiming to be some kind of lottery agent intent on offering the recipient a huge bundle of banknotes for doing absolutely nothing. Cassidy had sent him away with more than a flea in his ear, but at least they now knew he was home.

There was movement inside, and Withers took a small step back. First rule of standing on doorsteps: don't crowd your target. The door opened. "Yes?"

"Mr Cassidy? Paul Cassidy?"

"I am. Who…?"

"Forgive me, Mr Cassidy. My name is John Withers, and I'm sheriff of Bakerton. Could we have a chat, do you think?"

Cassidy blinked. "Is this about…?"

"Leroy Figgis, yes."

"Then please come in, sheriff." He led Withers through the small hall and turned left into a spacious lounge/diner, simply decorated in a man's style. No wife then, concluded Withers, as he was offered a dining chair at the table. Cassidy sat opposite, gazing at the cop over the top of his laptop. He made no effort to close it.

"I'm still coming to terms with this," Cassidy said, lines of worry playing across his forehead.

Withers studied the man. He was early forties, perhaps, with strong features and a square jaw. His nose looked a little crooked, like that of an amateur boxer, but his face was smooth, untouched by boxing glove or Botox. A winner, of course. Withers' sharp appraisal of Cassidy was confirmed by the range of black-and-white photographs which adorned most of one wall, showing a boxer in action or proudly displaying a trophy. The other man saw Withers' interest. "County champion for three years. Had hopes of the Olympics, but…"

"Injury?"

"Naw, I wish! My pa was killed in a road accident, so I became the breadwinner. No more time for amateur boxing. No more time for anything." He looked away wistfully.

"Sorry to hear that," said Withers.

"Water under the bridge, as they say."

There was a moment's silence, before Withers said, "You were Mr Figgis's private pilot?"

"Yes. For eight years. Good years."

"Ms Templeman says he was a fine employer."

"The best," Cassidy confirmed, before looking away.

Withers immediately felt there was something here. "To start with, I'm particularly interested in the events of four years ago, when you flew the group to Lanscarges."

Cassidy squirmed. "Do you think that's connected to Mr Figgis's death?"

"It's one line of our investigation, yes. How well did you know Fleming, Cameron and Baxter?"

"Not at all. I met them for the first time when they boarded the plane at Bakerton airstrip. That's where Mr Figgis worked from."

"I didn't realise that strip was used for international flights," said Withers in amazement. "It's no bigger than my back yard!"

Cassidy laughed. "It's probably a little bigger than that, but I know what you mean. Mr Figgis had aviation approval to use the strip for destinations up to five hundred miles distance."

"He greased a few palms, you mean?"

"Your words, sheriff..."

Withers nodded. "The island of Lanscarges is, what...?"

"Three hundred and seventeen miles away. An easy trip for his Pilatus."

"That's his plane?"

"Yes," said Cassidy, suddenly becoming much more animated. "It's a Pilatus PC-12 NG, built in Switzerland. A lot are used for cargo carrying, but Mr Figgis spent over a million kitting his out with everything he might need. She was a beauty."

Withers was getting involved now. "I can imagine. What was the flight to Lanscarges like?"

"With a cruising speed of five hundred km, we allowed a comfortable two hours for the flight, although the facilities on the island leave a lot to be desired. Very primitive – and that's putting it mildly."

"This particular flight, you had the four passengers…"

Cassidy sat back. "Oh, no. There were six."

Withers almost jumped. "Six? Who else was onboard?"

"Well," said Cassidy, "there was Mr Figgis, of course, and P, Nat and Ralphie… and the two other guys."

Withers thought he had been dropped into a slow-motion movie. Get on with it, man, his eyes beseeched.

"One was called Lucas…"

"Just Lucas?"

"That's all I ever heard. And the other went by the name of the General."

"What?"

"That's it. The General. A mean-looking bastard, too, if you don't mind me saying."

Withers didn't. "So, these two didn't work for the company?"

Cassidy threw back his head. "You must be joking! No, they were hired help, the heavies. Lucas didn't come over too bad – he spoke well and had respect for Mr Figgis, you could tell. The other guy, hell, he was his own man, no two ways about it. I was mighty glad when he didn't make the return flight."

"He stayed behind?" Withers was amazed. Who in their right mind would want to stay on that island when they had a luxury jet waiting for them?

"The others came back a couple of days later. I had to entertain myself on the plane all that time..."

"Tough life, but somebody's got to do it," sympathised Withers with a grin.

"Yeah, could have been a lot worse. Mr Figgis gave me carte blanche..."

"So, what were they like when they came back, the other five? Happy, celebrating a job well done, that sort of thing?" asked Withers.

"Far from it. They were pretty distressed, especially Ralphie, and Lucas was carrying a nasty cut to his neck. The funny thing was, though, they came back with nothing."

"What do you mean?"

"Well, on previous trips there had been boxes, crates, that sort of thing. But this time, zilch…"

"Were you expecting some kind of cargo?" asked Withers.

"Oh, yes. There was always something."

"But not this time."

Cassidy shook his head. "And… I'm sure there was somebody else onboard."

"Really? Who was it?" asked Withers, surprised.

Cassidy shrugged. "Haven't a clue, sheriff. I was sent to the cockpit before whoever it was boarded. Very mysterious."

"But it wasn't the General?"

"Oh, no. I'd recognise his cologne anywhere!"

"Could you describe this Lucas and the General?" asked Withers.

"Oh, yes."

Outside, Withers took out his phone. "Dawg, can you get a police artist over to Paul Cassidy's place, pronto?" He walked to his car, climbed in and mulled over everything he'd learnt. There had been six people on that jet; four of them were now dead, and two were at large, apparently capable of anything. Could these two be responsible, four years later, for the murders? It was the only lead he had. And there was one person who might possibly connect the dots and help him make a reasonable picture out of all this. It might not be correct police procedure, but he was going to do it anyway. He chose another number and waited for the connection. He had one more job for PA Grace Templeman.

Chapter Fifteen

Ty Cobden had no idea how to track down the General. Yesterday, he had walked the streets, just looking and thinking, without success at either enterprise. But he knew he couldn't do that indefinitely. He needed to be ahead of the killers, not following in their footsteps, unsure of which way to turn. He was getting frustrated.

He had watched the police station for a while, checking out the sheriff, his deputies, and the crowd of reporters camping out on the side of the street. He recognised a national TV presenter, her designer clothes making her stand out, as she accosted passers-by and thrust her microphone in their faces, demanding some kind of comment, no matter how banal or trivial. The viewers were lapping it up. What was there not to like? An investment banking heavyweight, slain in his home, along with a number of his acolytes – what a heady, intoxicating storyline that makes. It could run forever.

Ty had turned away then, sickened by it all. Thank God they didn't have all the hideous details.

The way Leroy had been butchered, cut to pieces by an animal not fit to live. The bile had risen in Ty's throat, and he had to get away.

Now he had found the lake: a beautiful, tranquil oasis in a world gone crazy. Ty had led a far from exemplary life, but he had been fond of Leroy and felt the loss bitterly. He sat on a bench and looked out over the water. There was a small yacht further out, the two occupants searching for wind as they turned the boat this way and that, the sail billowing and then sagging at each rotation. Ty wished he was with them – life would be so simple.

A man walking a dog passed by, the animal sniffing at Ty's leg. He bent down and stroked it, wondering what breed it might be. Looked like just a mongrel to him, but what did he know? The man nodded as he tugged the dog back into place beside him, and walked on, waving to someone else in the distance.

Ty took out the card he had found in the Colonial House and studied it without really looking at it. He again wondered how the Arsehole had gotten hold of his fingerprint. It was so clear. Lifted from his military records, he assumed. He was grateful that nobody had told the killer his new name, although even a cursory check of his birth certificate would offer up the possible answers. He thought of his mother, whose name he had now taken. She would be turning in her grave if she could see him now. She had been so proud when he joined up, telling everybody she met how he would be a hero. It hadn't quite worked out like that. Sure, he'd got a medal, but he'd also picked up a few mental issues, as you do. It had taken him months to come to terms with everything that had happened to him: the loss of close friends and the destruction of life and property. As Audie Murphy once said, war is a trip to hell and back. Now Ty was a wanted man, even if the authorities didn't know just yet who he was. It was only a matter of time.

He gave a last thought to Ralphie Baxter, who he'd had to kill to save himself, and rose from the bench. He took a final look at the sparkling water, sighed deeply, and moved on.

****

The two Defenders met up half an hour later. They drove on for a few more minutes until Leroy called a halt.

He gathered them together and waited for silence. "Gentlemen," he said softly, "thank you for your assistance. Now, you all know what is in these packages." He waited for their murmurs of assent to fade away. "I want you to unload the vehicles and make a pile of the packages over there." He pointed to an area behind them, where a deep hole had been dug. They looked confused. "Please, gentlemen, do as I say."

Without comment, they unloaded the Land Rovers and carried the packages to the edge of the hole, where they hesitated.

"Throw them in, if you will," instructed Leroy.

The General spun on his heel. "What are you doing?" he demanded.

"That is my business, my friend. You have done your job."

"No, no," the General spluttered. "This is valuable stuff. What are you going to do, bury it?"

"Oh, no," laughed Leroy, "far better than that. We are going to burn it!"

"You're insane!" screamed the General, tugging his rifle from his shoulder. Number Two, standing beside him, did the same, causing everybody else to freeze. It had been a spur-of-the-moment thing. The General had been under inflexible instructions, but he could see everything going down the pan. Did his contact know this shipment was going to be drugs? Was that why he targeted it? If so, he sure as hell didn't know what Leroy was going to do with it! "This lot is worth millions," he said, still unable to make sense of it all.

"Yes, it is," agreed Leroy. "But it is also a blot on humanity. It must be destroyed, before it kills people."

"You *are* insane!"

"I did wonder about you, my friend," said Leroy softly. "When you were recommended to me, I had my doubts. Tell me, how did you wheedle your way into this?"

The General laughed. "A friend in high places, Mr Figgis. Now, I would like you gentlemen to replace the packages. My colleagues and I will take good care of them." He pointed to Number Two and the two drivers, all of whom had their rifles trained on Leroy's group.

"A two million fee wasn't enough then," Leroy said.

"Not when I can have all of it. What is there here, ten, twenty million's worth?"

"On the streets, around sixteen million. If you get it onto the streets, that is," said Leroy, looking sideways at Lucas, hoping that he could do something about the situation. Lucas knew he couldn't, but also knew that he ought to try. He took a step forward, causing itchy trigger fingers to flex.

The General raised his arm and confronted Lucas. "I will not hesitate to kill you and your friends," he threatened, the chunky ring on his finger stroking Lucas's neck. Suddenly, with a swift swipe of his hand, he drew the ring across Lucas's skin, drawing blood and leaving a deep and nasty gash.

Lucas did not flinch. He just stood eyeballing the General, making it clear that only one of them was going to survive the day. "You'll be sorry for that," he said, his voice soft and sinister. The General smiled.

Under the barrels of several rifles, the group were forced to put the packages into the vehicles and then watched, helpless, as the General and his associates drove away, clearly heading for the coast, where they obviously hoped to secure a boat operated by a crooked captain. In a place like Lanscarges, that shouldn't be a problem. The island had a history of smuggling dating back to the golden age of the pirate, when Elizabethan privateers docked offshore and bartered with the locals to secure fine silks and casks of rum from the innumerable ships that had run aground off the island's rocky coastline – not to mention the local delicacy of Kinder goat's cheese, which soon became a staple of fashionable London.

Leroy squatted on the ground, defeated. Lucas sat beside him, a kerchief held to his neck. The bleeding had stopped, but the wound was still very tender.

"You were going to burn it?" asked Lucas, aghast.

"Of course," said Leroy. "It is a scourge on society."

"And you spent... how much?"

Leroy shrugged. "What with paying you guys, plus the drugs, around eighteen million."

"Just so you could burn it! Man, you *do* have more money than sense!"

"I make that in a year," said Leroy, without any semblance of swagger. "It's the least I can do."

There was nothing else to say.

Chapter Sixteen

The newspaper lay on the desk, unread. Withers was typing up a report – not that there was much to say. *No progress* means no progress, in any language. They couldn't even find the widow of the late Leroy Figgis the Fourth. They knew as much today as they did yesterday, and that was pretty near nothing. Figgis had been up to something, but what it was they were no nearer to finding out.

The door opened, and Rafferty came in carrying two coffees and a bag of cakes. "Hell," he laughed, "I must be the highest paid waiter in the country."

"Yeah," drawled Withers, "your boss should be so proud." He took the offered coffee and lifted the lid, sipping gingerly at the hot liquid. "Sugar?"

"No, sorry."

"Too bad. I must be on that diet again." He sipped silently.

"Cake?" asked Rafferty, eyeing the newspaper.

"You choose."

Rafferty picked up the paper and read the front page. He selected a cake and handed it to Withers.

"Excuse fingers," he said, and returned to scanning the paper.

The door opened again, and Dawg stepped in. "We've got something," he said excitedly. The other men looked at him. "Figgis had a brother... well, a half-brother, actually. On his mum's side."

Withers grunted. "The facts, Dawg, not a bloody family tree."

"Yes, boss. Well, this brother lived in Colville, that's a couple of hundred miles up country..."

Withers grunted again. "The facts, Dawg, not a bloody geography lesson!"

Dawg, suitably chastened, continued, "It seems that they were pretty close, these brothers. Figgis used to bail him out when he was in trouble – which was quite often, apparently." He looked at the notes he was carrying. "The brother, Frank, was a bit of a cokehead. Had a record for petty crime – a spot of shoplifting, that sort of thing – and was picked up a couple of times for peddling. Nothing too major."

Withers chewed this over. "So how come we didn't get this earlier?"

"Different name, boss. Frank was a Barber, not a Figgis. Nobody made the connection till now."

Rafferty was still looking at the paper, but he had been listening. "Do you think this is relevant, John?"

"I'm not sure."

Dawg was holding his breath. He had left the most important piece till last, and he wasn't sure how his boss would react. "There is one other thing... Frank Barber is dead."

He was getting that stare again. Withers finally said, "Now you decide to tell us that."

"Sorry. Er, Frank died of an overdose four years ago..."

"Around the time Figgis went to Lanscarges," mused Withers.

"A month or so before," agreed Dawg. "We also have reason to believe that Figgis was at Frank's bedside at the moment of his passing, and actually paid for the funeral. It was a pretty lavish affair by all accounts. Nothing was spared. They even had a carriage and horses for the..."

Withers grunted a third time. "Just the facts, Dawg, not a bloody obituary!"

****

Leroy sat for a long time, his head in his hands, despair on his face. Lucas studied his lord and master. He'd been with Leroy for a few years now; he had grown to respect and even like him as a friend and thought he knew him pretty well. But this was something else. He had never seen the man so dejected and lost. He placed his arm on Leroy's shoulder and waited.

Finally, Leroy spoke. "I've had enough, Lucas. This is the last trip. I used to get a buzz out of it all, picking up contraband goods and selling them on; but now..."

Lucas felt him shudder. "Forgive me, Leroy, but why the drugs this time? You've never touched them before. It's always been liquor or ivory or diamonds..."

Leroy looked at him. "All harmless things," he said, as if that exonerated him. "I made a profit, yes, but it was all about the thrill." He offered up a weak grin. "Life as a banker is pretty boring, I can tell you." After a pause, he added proudly, "All the money went to my foundation for disadvantaged kids, you know."

Lucas shifted his position, looking out at the others, who stood dumb-struck in a huddle, not sure what to do. "Did any of them know about the drugs?"

Leroy shook his head vigorously. "Certainly not! Even Pandando was shocked when I enquired about the possibility. Although I knew he would be able to secure them for me."

"So, what's with the idea of burning them?" It was the question Lucas had been desperate to ask.

Leroy sighed heavily. "Long story. But let me just say, I did it for Frank."

Of course, that made no sense to Lucas, but he knew he had to do something. He gripped Leroy's arm. "Listen, we can still get the stuff back. Call Pandando, get him to send over a truck pronto. It's going to take the General a while to find a willing boat owner. We can still cut him off. Now, get off your arse and do something!"

Leroy was stunned. Nobody had ever spoken to him like that before, and he didn't know how to react. All his life he had been shown nothing but respect, and now this man was hollering at him, *ordering* him! He looked at Lucas, at the man's blazing eyes and throbbing temple, and he saw a caged animal trying to break free, desperate to go hunting. Lucas put his hand on Leroy's shoulder and squeezed, as if imparting his energy into the fallen man. Leroy responded.

"You're right," he said, his voice booming across the clearing, making the others turn to look at him. "You're right, Lucas! Let's do this!"

Re-energised, they both rose and began preparations for revenge...

****

When the office was finally empty, Withers picked up the newspaper and flicked through it. He had told himself not to, but he never listened to anybody, so why on earth should he listen to himself?

There was a lot of pure speculation and blatant lies about the killings, as to be expected, but Withers found a couple of interesting and pertinent articles, one of which carried the byline 'By our correspondent on the spot, Judith Wiseman'. He read through it, trying to find something to dislike about it. There was nothing, and he felt almost relieved. He read it again.

After several moments of indecision, he picked up his phone and dialled the *Oracle* office. "Hi, this is Sheriff John Withers in Bakerton." He waited for an acknowledgement, then said, "Look, I appreciate that Judith Wiseman isn't in the office..." The girl on the other end pointed out, with not a little humour, that Judith might, quite possibly, be down in the street below his office. "Yes," he agreed, "I'm sure she is. Look, can you just get her to give me a call, please?" When he put down the receiver, he really wished he hadn't done that.

****

By all accounts, the guy was weird. Judith reclined on her bed, her heels kicked off haphazardly onto the floor, sheets of A4 all around her, the portable printer on the desk still churning out more documents for her to get her teeth into. Rose at the office had worked wonders, delving deep into the archives for anything at all relating to Raymond Ross – and there was a lot of it, all emailed over and now seemingly spurting out of the printer at a rate almost as fast as the *Oracle*'s fastest web press.

Judith had tried to put it all into some semblance of order, but that was beyond even her. So, she just dipped into the pile, drawing out things that looked interesting or pertinent; and the sum total was that Mister Ross was a strange kettle of fish altogether. Testimonials by so-called friends read almost like the result of a legal subpoena, where they had been forced to testify, but they sure as hell didn't want to! Their praise was faint indeed, and it was perfectly clear that Raymond would not become the May Queen this or any other year.

Judith pulled out one sheet and studied it. A quote from an old college buddy from way back: 'Ray had few friends, but he knew how to work his way to the top. The rest of us just became his stepping stones.' *Nice*. She really needed to meet this man and get inside him.

But before she could reach for her phone, it began to sing to her with a ringtone of the overture from *West Side Story*, her favourite musical of all time. She picked it up and fell back onto the bed. On the other end was Yvette from the office, giggling like a girl and cooing sweet nothings about the local sheriff wanting to arrest her and put her in handcuffs.

Judith put down the phone, a smile forming on her face and a tingle developing a little lower...

****

The diner was busy, but Millie Moody had been given time off. She had taken a call from a friend of her Aunt Faith, who told her that Faith was poorly and was asking for her. She thought it was unusual, because Faith lived a bus ride away, and she didn't often get in touch. Still, the man had been insistent, and he seemed to know all about Faith and her daughter, April, even mentioning the tragic loss of her husband, Jim.

Millie cleaned the last table and took off her apron. While the regular customers were buzzing, there hadn't been so many reporters in today – they'd migrated to the McDonald's or the Chicken Shack around the corner. No loss, she thought. Reporters don't tip.

Putting on her coat, she said goodbye to Scott, the owner, and stepped out into the street, looking up to see if the sheriff was peeking at her. She knew he often took a quick look, but it meant nothing. In fact, she felt somehow safer with the knowledge, and next time he came round to play chess with her pa, she'd rib him about his ogling. She smiled to herself, turned left and began walking down Prenton Street.

She didn't notice the swarthy man behind her.

****

The General could contain himself no longer. He phoned the number he had been told never to use, and waited. It took half a minute before it was answered.

"It's me," said the General.

"What the hell! You know what I said about this number. Only to be used in extreme emergencies." A pause. "So, what's the emergency?"

"I need to know what's going on," said the General.

"You what? Jesus, man, are you crazy? Haven't I done enough for you?"

"Not as much as I've done for you," pointed out the General, with an edge to his voice.

"Look, I've got you Lucas's fingerprints, and I've given you details of the Moody family. Not to mention the money…"

"Yeah, and what have I done for you, eh?" screamed the General.

"Not over the phone. Don't say another word. I'm discontinuing this discussion. Listen to me," the voice was at once strong and authoritative, "this finishes now. You went too far with... you just went too far. Do not contact me again. Do you understand?"

The General snarled, "We'll see about that!" and threw his phone against the wall, a large patch of plaster breaking off and joining the phone on the floor.

DAY FOUR

Chapter Seventeen

They met for breakfast at the diner: neutral ground. The place looked as if it had been modelled on the set of *Happy Days*, all fifties stainless steel panels, terrazzo marble floor and Formica tables in a rainbow of colours, each with matching bench seats and overhanging art nouveau lighting. Framed pictures of fifties icons like James Dean, Marilyn Munroe and King Elvis adorned the walls, all painted by a local artist with a flair for nostalgia mixed with cutting-edge modernity. It was not to everyone's taste, but then you only went in there for sustenance. For culture, you'd go to the small gallery in the art shop down the road.

The waitress offered them a table in an alcove, which they took. He was mildly surprised Millie hadn't rushed out to see him with this woman. He knew very well that she would have been fascinated and shocked in equal measure to see him with someone.

When the waitress came back, she took their order: he was having poached egg on rye with overflowing coffee – he needed more than one cup this time of the morning. She chose brown-bread toast, low-fat spread, and a large hot chocolate, complete with marshmallows and a cocoa sprinkle. She'd bowed to her fitness instructor by having the low-fat spread, but she sure as hell wasn't going to miss out on the luxury of the hot chocolate. Besides, either she was going to claim it on expenses, or he would be settling the bill.

They sat in silence until the food arrived. She took the time to study her companion. She had liked what she saw from the first meeting, but knew that he could be an almost impenetrable character. She had to tread very carefully if this relationship was to have a chance. To be honest, she'd never experienced this kind of stirring before, and she hoped he felt the same.

As the waitress returned with the tray, Judith looked around the diner. "Nice place," she said, with the waitress not sure she was talking to her. She gave a little sound which might have been 'Thanks', then withdrew.

Withers broke his egg and was rewarded with a good amount of runny yolk. "Yes, it is," he said, "and the eggs are great, too."

They ate in more silence before Judith felt the time was right. "Thanks for this."

"What? Breakfast? I assumed you'd put it on expenses."

So now she knew! "That's fine. The *Oracle* has deep coffers. But actually, I meant thanks for talking to me again." He nodded and offered her a smile, as she swirled her marshmallows and took a spoonful, savouring the taste as they melted in her mouth. "I do love these," she said.

"So I see."

Was that a criticism? Was he judging her? "So," she began, "here we are."

"Yes. Enjoy."

A man of few words. Judith bit into her toast and chewed, both physically and mentally. She couldn't make this man out. True, he had a complex murder case to contend with, but there must be a way for her to get through to him. However, whatever she did, she didn't want to mention the case. "So, how's it going?" Damn.

"What? Life?"

Oh, he was so obtuse! "The case, silly."

"Ah, the case."

He wasn't making things easy for her. "Off the record, of course."

He sipped his coffee, eyeing her as he did so. My, but she was beautiful! "Slowly."

A bit like this conversation, thought Judith wistfully. "Why was Figgis targeted, do you think? Robbery's been discounted, I assume."

Withers gave the slightest of nods. "Definitely not robbery."

"You haven't released much to the press."

"No, I haven't."

Judith took another mouthful of her toast and waited.

Withers pushed away his empty plate and wiped his mouth on the napkin, folding it neatly after he had finished. He reached for his cup but stopped mid-way. "I owe you an explanation."

Judith stopped chewing. "Do you?" she asked, small pieces of toast coming to the edge of her mouth. He so wanted to wipe them away… and kiss her!

"You referred to a 'significant other'," he said.

"In your office, yes, I did. I'm sorry if that…"

"No," he interrupted, putting his hand on hers, and then leaving it there for a moment. She made no effort to move. "It's a painful story."

She saw the hurt in his eyes and put her other hand on his and squeezed gently. "You don't have to tell me, you know?"

"Oh," he said, putting his hand on the others, making a full tower, "I think we both know that I have to."

Wow, all of a sudden it was happening so quickly. Judith took a deep breath, knowing that what was to come would define their relationship forever. "If you think it will help."

Withers seemed to take a step back. "Do you want another drink? More toast?"

"I'm fine." Her eyes were begging him to unburden himself. He could see it.

"My 'significant other' was... Heather. My wife."

She pulled her hand out from the bottom of the pile and put it on top, squeezing his hand again. She said nothing.

"We'd been married for eight years – she would have told you she was a teenage bride!" They both laughed nervously. "I'd got a job... in the city, where we were living then. I'm a country boy, really, but I needed to go where the money was. Bad move." He hesitated, remembering. "Some lowlife broke into the flat, and when Heather came back, she obviously disturbed him." Long, long pause. "So, he knifed her."

Judith couldn't hold back a gasp. "I'm so sorry, John."

She hadn't used his first name before, but he liked it. "I found her when I got home. He'd left her where she fell. Doctors said it took several hours for her to pass." His voice grew angry. "I should have been there!"

"You were on duty, John," Judith offered as some kind of comfort.

"No, you've got it wrong," he said, his voice cracking. "I wasn't a cop then. I worked for a printing company. Driving."

"Okay," she persevered, "so you were at work."

"But that's the point," he said, his eyes so watery that he could see nothing. "I wasn't working. I'd gone fishing with a couple of pals."

"You can't blame yourself." Judith's words sounded hollow to him. "You *mustn't* blame yourself."

"I shouldn't have told you."

"I'm glad you did. Now I can help you work through it."

Withers did not answer, so she just held his hand. They sat there for several minutes, the spell of Heather binding them, while at the same time splitting them. Judith wasn't sure if she wanted to fight the memory of a deceased wife, but what choice did she really have? John Withers had stepped into her heart and was at this moment twisting it, through no fault of his own, and without realising the damage he was causing. She sighed heavily, and he gave her a weak smile.

"Coffee always does the trick," he said, almost believing it. "Heals all wounds."

She called over the waitress. "Please can you top up my friend's coffee – and I'll have a skinny latte."

Judith felt devastated but could do nothing but be there for him. She continued to stroke his hand, even though she knew he could no longer feel it, lost as he was in the distant past.

Chapter Eighteen

It had been wet when he left Lanscarges – almost at tropical monsoon level, with the wind howling noisily through the trees and the birds squawking with fear at the violent onrush of wind and debris, as bins were overturned, and rubbish swept through the empty streets.

It was hot, too. Far above the seasonal norm, as the local radio station had been quick to point out. He always sweated badly in the heat and was embarrassed at the huge patches of damp which invariably spread over his shirt at times like this.

He'd been lucky to have hitched a ride from the island to the mainland on a fishing boat. The boat had been stifling, too, and he was so grateful to have sunk several long, cool drinks offered to him by a member of the crew. It had cost him an arm and a leg, but at least then he could catch a plane to his destination, even if it did mean a long taxi ride to the airport at Delcine first. After all that, this hop to Altona International Airport was a piece of cake.

Pandando could, at last, relax in his seat as he chewed over the phone call. Leroy's PA, by the name of Grace, he recalled, had explained at some length the passing of her boss, and Pandando had offered suitable lamentations and sympathetic words. He'd heard about it, of course, and had been surprised, like everyone else, but he had no feelings either way. Leroy was, after all, just an associate. Nevertheless, he did wonder...

This Grace had then told him that he stood to gain something if he could get himself over to the bank in Bakerton at his earliest convenience. He had quizzed her on the details, without success, so told her that he would be over as soon as possible, and that he would phone her back when he had made the arrangements. He thought she had been a bit sharp then, when she had told him that she would book his flight for the next day. All he had to do was turn up at Delcine airport at midday and pick up his ticket. He was a little put out by being dictated to in this way, but he was far more annoyed that the huge Mercurial Bank had not sent Leroy's private jet to collect him. Tight-wads, he seethed, at the same time drooling at the prospect of getting something for nothing at the end of the day.

The plane was wonderfully cool, and he was pleased that his shirt no longer had the tell-tale stains. He clasped his pudgy fingers together in his lap and looked past the woman in the next seat to the view through the window. It was a glorious day, with the sun high in the sky and no clouds to speak of. As the plane began to descend, he saw the great Bluestone Mountains come into sight, and was fascinated by the shadow of the plane as it passed over the peaks, growing bigger and then getting smaller as each peak was climbed and passed.

The nice young stewardess asked passengers to fasten their seatbelts, and he felt the slightest of shudders as the plane smoothly descended beyond the mountains and the airport came into view below. He grinned to himself, and the woman beside him gave him a look so damning that he mumbled an apology and looked away.

He had never been to Altona. Why should he? He had conducted all his work on the island and had no need to leave it. But this was different. Leroy had been the biggest thing to ever happen to him, and there could be something in this. He had always been fair to Leroy, and he hoped that the bank man had a soft spot for him.

They had met through a mutual friend when Leroy visited the island to purchase some land for development. They had clicked immediately, enjoying drinks in his local bar and talking business until all hours, before Pandando introduced him to the delights of his club. The men were a perfect match, and it hadn't taken long for the subject of 'less than legal' transactions to come up. Both were more than happy to go down this route, and Leroy had visited several times to cement the association… until the last time, four years ago.

Pandando made his way to the exit. He only had a holdall, so there was no formal check on him. He blinked as the sun filtered through the glass panels of the Arrivals lounge, and then he tried to get his bearings. His eye caught a tall, well-built man dressed in a smart black suit and wearing a chauffeur's peaked cap. He held up a placard with Pandando's name on it.

"That's me," Pandando said, and the man grunted some sort of acknowledgement and turned to leave, so Pandando quickly followed, worried that he might lose him. His fat little legs barely kept up with the chauffeur.

The driver got into a black limo but made no effort to open the door for his passenger. Pandando was about to say something but thought better of it. He climbed into the car and threw his holdall onto the seat. "Nice place," he said, although he hadn't even had time to take a look around. He just thought he ought to make conversation. The driver nodded slightly, before driving into the traffic.

Pandando nestled into the rich upholstery of the luxury car and looked out of the window. He was used to living on the edge of a jungle, so all of this was an awakening to him. Could he live like this, surrounded by other human beings at close proximity? No, that was the simple answer; he'd stay where he belonged, thanks very much.

The car was travelling at a fair pace, seemingly not taking too much notice of street directions and pedestrians. This guy was sure in a hurry.

When they flashed past the sign proclaiming the 'Rustic town of Bakerton', Pandando began to get a little excited. He had tried not to think about what Leroy may have left him, because he was basically a cautious man, and, some might say, pretty pessimistic. But he had high hopes...

He studied the driver, who didn't seem the kind of person a renowned bank might employ. He had not shown any respect for his passenger, and he had uttered not a word since their journey had begun. Pandando tutted to himself. Man, you just can't get the staff these days. He thought he would mention this to Grace when he met her. The bank needed to know that their staff were not up to the job. He looked out the window again, seeing for the first time the deep blue of a large lake, shimmering in the afternoon sun. *Beautiful.*

The car came to an abrupt halt, and Withers got out, throwing the peaked cap back onto the passenger seat. After his breakfast with Judith and the raking over of the still-warm embers of his past, he was ready for anything now, and this punk was going to feel the full force. He opened the rear door. "Get out," he ordered, tapping his breast at an imaginary holster. Pandando, shocked, did not move. "I said, get out!" Withers roared, causing the other man to slink back in his seat. Withers slid his hand inside his jacket, and suddenly Pandando was in a racing hurry to comply with the request. He scuttled out, almost falling to the ground.

"Okay," he muttered, confused. "I'm out! Don't shoot!"

Withers patted the inside of his jacket for effect, then withdrew his hand, grabbing Pandando by the collar and dragging him to a picnic bench a few feet away. He plonked the man down, then hovered over him, glowering. "Tell me about Leroy Figgis."

Pandando had regained a little of his spirit. "Who the hell are you, man? What's this all...?"

"Figgis. Talk to me about him."

Pandando blinked first. "What about Leroy? He's an associate, that's all. Well, he was, cos I heard the news."

"Yeah," said Withers, "gone in a puff." He wasn't sure whether he was over-playing the hard man act, but it was too late now. He leaned in closer. "How did you know Figgis?"

"He came to see me a few times…"

"Business or pleasure?" Withers sneered, starting to enjoy his role-playing.

"Oh, business… always business."

"What kind?"

Pandando wanted so desperately to lie, but he didn't like the look of this big guy; plus, he didn't know what he already knew. "You know."

"Pretend I don't."

"Look, man, I'll call a cop!"

Withers scrunched up Pandando's collar and looked around. They're closer than you think, he thought to himself. "I don't see no cops," he whispered in the other man's ear, "so keep talking."

Pandando gulped. "He told me he had a few clients who, you know… well, they liked to… er, snort." His little bloodshot eyes looked up. "But you must know that, surely?"

"I like it straight from the horse's mouth. How much are we talking? Not recreational, I assume."

Pandando was beginning to twig. "Hold on. Who in hell's garden *are* you? I'm not saying another word."

Withers was annoyed with himself. "Let's talk about Lucas…"

"No."

"Or the General." He saw the slightest twitch at the corner of Pandando's mouth and knew he had him. "The thought of him frighten you, Mr Pandando?"

"No," he replied, his voice trembling just slightly.

"I have it on good authority that this General is a real motherfucker. Know what I mean?" He could see Pandando knew *exactly* what he meant. "So where is he?"

"I don't know – honestly."

"He didn't come back with Figgis all those years ago. Why was that?" Withers put his hand inside his jacket, and Pandando recoiled.

"They had some kind of an argument, him and Leroy, so I heard."

"About?"

"That's all I know. The rest of the guys came back from the jungle without him. They said he'd been killed…"

"But we know he hadn't."

"Yeah. One of my men told me afterwards that he'd been wounded but had survived." Pandando paused, a glimmer of hope appearing in his eyes. "Hey, man, is that it? You're working for Leroy's people to get at the General."

"Wrong and right," said Withers. "What about Lucas?"

Pandando couldn't stop talking now. "He was Leroy's man. Tough, too. Ex-military, I would say.

Him and the General didn't see eye to eye from the beginning. I wasn't surprised only one of them came back. Mind you, bud, I would have put money on the General. Mean bastard." He stopped, hoping that he had spilled enough beans. But Withers wasn't letting him off the hook that easily.

"How much snort are we talking, Vincent?"

Pandando was surprised to hear the man use his given name. "Er, industrial quantities, friend. Leroy had the perfect carrier – his jet."

And the perfect cover, being a respected banker, thought Withers, pleased that it was all beginning to fall into place. "Where did it come from, originally?"

"Look, if it means you're gonna get that madman General, I'll tell you everything. It was shipped in to Lanscarges by fishing boats off Columbian freighters. Leroy flew in to buy it. I gave him the heads-up, and he went in to collect it." He paused. "I'll deny all this, if necessary."

"No problem, Vincent. I don't intend you to go to court."

Pandando felt the shakes in his legs. Was that a threat, or a promise? What the hell was he getting into? "You're not going to hurt me, are you?"

"Not yet, maybe not ever. Who knows?"

With that, Withers reached into the car, pulled out Pandando's holdall and threw it at him. The bag almost knocked him off balance. "Hey, man, what are you doing? I need to get to the Mercurial Bank – they've got somethin' for me."

Withers grinned. "I've got something for you, Vincent. A word of advice. Forget about the bank, Leroy and everything else. Go back to your little island hole and stay there. If I hear another bleat out of you... *ever*... it's farewell, my lovely. Understand?"

Pandando looked puzzled. *Farewell, my lovely*? What...? "Yeah, understood. Thanks for nothin', pal." He shouldered the holdall and watched as Withers climbed into the car and pulled away.

Withers smirked to himself as Pandando disappeared in the rear-view mirror. Time to return the car to his old friend Casey, who runs the town's limousine-hire company.

****

The old truck rumbled into view, and Lucas took a double-take. "Bloody hell, Leroy, is that the best they had?"

Leroy shrugged. "Beggars can't be choosers, Lucas. Pandando wanted enough for it as it was."

"Let's hope it does the job!" Lucas half-joked, as he greeted the driver. He looked in the cab and pulled out a sub-machine-gun, playing with it lovingly.

171

"And they cost even more than the truck," said Leroy.

Lucas handed one of the machine-guns to Nat – who didn't look too thrilled at the prospect – gave Ralphie a rifle and took possession of the other sub-machine-gun from the cab. "Now we're ready!"

The others climbed into the open back of the truck, while Lucas sat in the cab. He had seamlessly taken command of the unit, and Leroy was happy with that. He was thinking only of the damage to humanity all that dope could inflict.

They made slow progress, partly because of the sluggishness of both the truck and the driver, and partly because of the rough terrain over which they were travelling. It was not a comfortable ride.

****

The office was too warm, but Withers didn't like his door open, so Rafferty stood by the half-open window, drawing in as much of the slight breeze as he could. He turned to Withers, who sat at the desk, scanning some files. "I don't think my boss is going to be too impressed with the way you're operating, John."

"I work my own way."

Rafferty moved over and leant on the desk. "I understand... but I'm not sure she will."

"Tough."

Rafferty smiled. "You wouldn't say that to her face."

Withers looked up. "Wouldn't I?"

"Not unless you want one of your testicles suspended from that light fitting…"

"Really?"

"And the other one wrapped around that doorknob – with you still attached to both." Rafferty laughed. "Now that I would love to see!"

"Okay, Pat, I get how you feel, but I do my own thing."

Rafferty softened. "Fair enough. So, what have we got?"

Withers eyed the other man, then smiled. "*We* have got quite a lot, actually. Let's take it from the beginning. Leroy Figgis, billionaire, runs what could be a lucrative sideline in drug-running…"

"Why would he do that?"

"Who knows… power, the sense of adventure, because he can? Or perhaps he had been supplying his half-brother Frank?" Withers looked at his notes. "Four years ago, on the same day, his bank employed: *one*, Piers Fleming, who just happens to be fluent in Spanish. *Two*, Nathaniel Cameron, a long-standing acquaintance of Figgis who is also fluent in Spanish. *Three*, Ralph Baxter, a young man with

173

potential as the biggest yes-man in history. He'd do anything Figgis told him to do."

"Yes, but we knew all that," said Rafferty with a frown.

"*Four*, Lucas somebody, probably ex-military, and Figgis' strong right arm."

Rafferty looked impressed. "That's good."

"*Five*, a guy who calls himself the General…"

"You kidding me?"

Withers ignored him. "The General is the complete unknown. We don't know where Figgis found him, but he was definitely the second heavy in the group. Now…" He was really getting into gear now. "They all took a flight in Figgis's private jet to Lanscarges, which is a mainly Spanish-speaking island three hundred miles away."

"I know it. Got some stunning coastline," commented Rafferty.

"Perfect for fishing vessels to sail in and out filled with Columbian drugs, as well. Anyway, the group met up with Vincent Pandando, a creepy little go-between, who directed them inland to the stock of drugs. I presume they then negotiated with a third person, before bringing the drugs back to the jet."

"Sounds too easy."

"Yes," agreed Withers, "but something went wrong. It appears that this General didn't make it.

Somebody, perhaps Lucas Somebody, tried to kill him."

"But he didn't?" said Rafferty.

"No. Vincent Pandando assures me that the General is still alive."

Rafferty stepped back. "Hold it, John. You spoke to this Pandando guy?"

"I did."

"You haven't had time to go to this island."

"I thought it might be prudent to invite him here."

"What? Is he in a cell?"

"Sorry, Pat, but I couldn't arrest him."

Rafferty was almost speechless. "It sounds like he as good as confessed, John."

"True... but there might have been a little, er, *coercion* on my part." Withers winked. "What he told me would never stand up in court, so I had to let him go. For now."

"Hell, man... perhaps it was lucky you didn't tell me what you were up to," said Rafferty, slapping the sheriff on the back.

"Rules are never straight lines, Pat. They can quite often go round corners," said Withers, finally relaxing in Rafferty's company. It had been a strained relationship, but now that the Irishman had accepted his way of working, Withers felt more at ease. Perhaps it won't be too bad after all. He continued,

"There is one more thing, Pat. Six people went out, and six people came back…"

"But not the General."

"No. The pilot, Paul Cassidy, was sure that six people got on the plane, but Figgis kept the last person hidden from view. Cassidy was not able to tell me who it might have been. But he was adamant that it wasn't the General."

"Intriguing," said Rafferty, "and where is this General now?"

"Who knows? Is he the mysterious assassin, or the second killer… or nobody of importance?" said Withers, unable to answer his own question.

****

Lucas had had enough. He ordered the driver to pull over, then took the wheel himself. With little thought for the consequences, he gunned the pedal until the throaty roar of the Second World War engine turned into a desperate cry for help. Leroy and the others clung on for dear life, cursing the driver and retching over the side, as the truck hurtled round the mountain road and on towards the coast, every boulder and crevice shaking its very soul.

Lucas was sickened at the way Leroy had been treated. It was time to fight back. The islander sitting beside him was gripping the door handle and mumbling in incoherent Spanish, praying for salvation from the *hombre loco* and his death machine. Nobody was safe from the wrath of this mad driver.

****

"We've got her," beamed Dawg, as he peered round the door.

"Christine Figgis?" asked Withers.

"Er, not exactly. They weren't married."

Withers beckoned his deputy in and pointed to a seat. Dawg took it, flattered that he was on the same level as his boss. "She'd been hiding out at a cheap hotel. But we picked her up at the international airport, about to jump on a budget flight to Europe."

Budget, thought Withers; with all that money, she still tries to flee on a budget ticket.

"She is happy to talk. I think she is scared, boss."

Withers nodded. "Not surprising, considering what happened to her, um, boyfriend."

"Her name is Christina Hernandez…"

"Spanish," stated Withers.

"Yes, boss."

"From Lanscarges."

Dawg raised his eyes. "*Yes*, boss."

"The mysterious sixth passenger, I wouldn't wonder."

Dawg was stunned. "Yes, boss."

"Go on."

"Well, she says that she had been having an affair with Figgis for several years. He was kind and considerate, and a great lover, and…"

"Okay, Dawg, this isn't *Cosmopolitan* magazine."

"Right, boss." Dawg paused. "She says he smuggled her onboard his jet…"

"An illegal," Withers mused.

"It would seem so, boss."

"Well then, let's go and see what else she has to say, shall we?"

Withers was not expecting the woman who sat at the table in the interview room. To say she was stunning would be most unfair. Her jet-black hair fell loosely over her high cheekbones and deep-set blue eyes, so large that they reminded Withers of the Western Lake. She did not appear to have the slightest Hispanic blood in her, her skin being pale and smooth. Her trim figure was hugged by a powder-blue three-quarter-length pair of slacks which left no room for a panty-line, deep blue sling-back sandals and a tight-fitting white t-shirt bearing a blood-red rose over her left breast. The rose was, one might say, blooming. She watched silently as Withers and Dawg entered and took the seats opposite her. There was silence for a few seconds, as Withers got his breath back. Dawg just blushed.

"Miss Hernandez…" Withers started.

"Before you begin, sheriff," she said in perfect English, "I would like to ask for protection."

Withers waited. He knew she would open up, so why not just let her run?

"I know that my Leroy was murdered by the General. Logically, I am next."

"And why would that be?" asked Withers.

"Because he will get me on his way to Lucas."

Dawg had started the tape before the conversation began and was also taking notes. Now, he looked up. He wanted to ask something, but Withers held up his hand and said to her, "Please, Miss Hernandez, can we start at the beginning?"

"You will protect me?" she repeated, and Withers nodded, while Dawg scribbled the fact on his pad. She continued, "I met Leroy six, seven years ago. I worked for a Vincent Pandando on…"

"Yes, we know him," Withers said.

"It was a 'house of fun', Vincent called it. I am sure you will have other names." She gave a short, hoarse laugh. "Leroy became my patron. He insisted that I went with no other men, and he made it worthwhile for both me and Vincent. I was faithful."

Dawg rolled his eyes. He'd heard everything now.

"Leroy came over several times, and I looked forward to it. He was a lovely man, sheriff." Her breath caught in her throat, and a tear appeared in one eye. She dabbed at it with a dainty lace handkerchief. "A present from Leroy," she said, waving it. "It will never leave me."

Despite his hard-nosed experience, Withers actually believed her. After all, Figgis had rescued her and set her up for life.

As if reading his mind, Christina said, "It is all I have left. Leroy gave me a handsome allowance, of course, and I lived in his mansion… but now there is nothing. No yachts, no offshore accounts, nothing. It all died with him." She smiled wanly. "I am not bitter, sheriff, apart from losing the man I truly loved."

Withers waited for her to calm down, before saying, "So what exactly happened, Miss Hernandez?"

"Firstly, my name is not Hernandez. It is Gonzalez. Leroy's housekeeper was my mother."

Dawg and Withers exchanged looks. "Go on," pressed Withers.

"My mother knew that Leroy was operating some kind of business on Lanscarges, so she asked him to find me and save me. And that is what he did." Christina asked for a glass of water and waited while Dawg poured it for her. She took it and drank the glass dry, before continuing, "It took Leroy some time to find me, and he then had to soften up Vincent in order to get me out. It was not easy."

Withers said, "It was probably easier than you think, seeing as Pandando and Figgis were in partnership."

"Leroy did not like Vincent. He tolerated him… for me," Christina insisted, rocking on her chair. She was still in shock.

"Let's talk about your mother. Did this General know you two were related?"

"I think he suspected. But whatever he knew or didn't know, he had to get rid of my mother because she could recognise him. Like me, she was on his hit list."

Withers could see that Christina was not overwhelmed with grief over the loss of her mother. "You were not close," he stated, watching for a reaction.

Christina shuddered. "You think I am a callous woman, sheriff?"

"Are you?"

She thought about that one for a few seconds. "I suppose I am. My mother knew that Leroy was a lonely man and she hoped he would fall for me. She thought she could use this to her own ends. What she did not expect, though, was that I fell in love with him. And I saw right through her plan. That is why she remained only his housekeeper. She resented that fact."

One thing had always nagged Withers: there had been no sign of forced entry at the Colonial House. It almost appeared as if the killers had been invited in. "You say that your mother knew the General."

"Yes," Christina replied. "She told me that he had come to the house on several occasions while they were planning the trip. Why?"

Withers had no intention of sharing his thoughts with her, but it now seemed likely that her mother had willingly opened the door, probably in the false hope of some kind of payment, and possibly not knowing what the General had planned. Or perhaps she did know, and that was why, as she walked away, the General had silenced her for good.

"No reason," he said, his face passive and revealing nothing. "I will arrange a safe house for you, Miss Gonzalez."

"Thank you, sheriff. But please call me Mrs Figgis. It is not legal, I know, but it is all I have."

Withers understood, and he sat in silence as Dawg guided her from the room. Oh, yes, he understood about loss…

Chapter Nineteen

The Heights had been aptly named, commanding, as it did, a panoramic view over the thirty-nine other properties which made up Copper Ridge West. Created by award-winning architect Marvin Franklin fifty years previous, the houses, bungalows and cabins had been lovingly crafted in man-made clearings between the beautiful tall copper birch trees.

It had taken a herculean effort to get sanitation pipes and electricity cables up to the Ridge, but Marvin was a consummate organiser, and his team of craftsmen would have followed him to the end of the earth if that had been on his blueprint. The result was a remarkable collection of high-class dwellings in a staggeringly wonderful setting. And Marvin was going to have the cream of them, the prize for all the hard work both he and his wife Martha had put into those six years. It was their Garden of Eden.

Martha had wanted to call their place *Wuthering Heights* when they first moved in. But Marv had thought there might be a copyright problem with the

Brontë estate – after all, he was an architect, not a copyright expert – so Martha had compromised, and their beautiful new three-storey house had been named *The Heights*.

Her Marv had been gone for nearly thirty years now, taken from her by the big C. She had nursed him through the most awful months of her life, as she watched him disappear from her on a daily basis – first his movements, then that wonderful straw-coloured hair that she so loved to stroke, until, finally, he lost his voice, his reason, his life…

Martha was on the verandah, her battered old hat shielding her eyes from a strong but still watery morning sun. Now well into her eighties, she counted her blessings that she was still able to live in the house and move freely. She had thought again of her Marv.

She folded the newspaper she had been reading, drained her glass of iced lemon barley, and rose a little unsteadily, before making her way into her upside-down house. To get the most out of the view, Marv had cleverly put the office on the ground, the bedrooms on the first, and a massive lounge and kitchen up top, complete with wide French windows opening onto the large verandah.

Martha made for the office. It was funny, but she still thought of it as Marv's study, and every time she opened the door, she could almost see him sitting at his desk or his architect's easel, and she was sure she got a whiff of the tobacco from his pipe. He didn't light it often, preferring to just suck on it as he worked, or chew on it if he had a particularly troubling problem to wrestle with. Martha had left the pipe on his desk as a permanent reminder – as if she needed such a thing – of what she had lost.

She moved over to the far wall, which was completely covered by a map of the complex, each house beautifully drawn as if a photograph had been taken and stuck on the paper. It had been Marv's idea. He had wanted to build a communal hall of some kind, so that his map could be on permanent display, along with other artefacts, such as the bones they found when setting the foundations. An expert had said they were at least a thousand years old, and Marv had got quite excited. However, the developers called a halt to any further expansion, which meant that all the finds were entrusted to the museum in Bakerton – and his map stayed at *The Heights*.

Martha, in Marv's image, had painstakingly kept the map up to date by filling in the owners as they came and went. There were only two names for *The Heights*, of course, one sadly crossed out, but some properties had changed hands several times over the years, and now she took up her red felt-tip and put a line through one name, adding, in green, the date of four days ago. She sighed heavily and put the pens down, before sitting at the desk, checking a number she had previously written on a large pad in front of her, and reaching for the phone.

****

It had been a quiet morning. Dawg was even doodling on a scrap of paper he'd taken from the waste-bin. The sheriff and Rafferty were out some place, and the other deputies were patrolling. He'd drawn the short straw and was manning the office.

The shrill of the telephone caused him to drop his pen, and he scrambled on the floor for it, at the same time grabbing the phone. "Deputy Doug Janowski," he mumbled, somewhat breathlessly.

"Douglas?" a voice enquired.

Dawg sat up immediately. "Mrs Franklin? Hi, how are you this morning?" He loved Martha Franklin. She could have been his gran, or very close to it. And she was a great citizen. Never mind Neighbourhood Watch; she was Martha Watch. He was sitting comfortably, pen retrieved, when she began.

"I've read the newspaper." She was a notoriously slow starter. "About that poor Mr Figgis; you know, the banking magnate. Shocking."

"Yes, it is," agreed Dawg.

"But there was something else, Douglas."

Dawg knew this might be important. Martha Franklin didn't do mundane. "What is that, Mrs Franklin?"

"One of those poor unfortunates – you know, the ones who were with him…"

"Yes?"

"He was a Mr Ralph Baxter."

Dawg wasn't sure whether this was a question or not. "He was."

"He leased a property up here, on Copper Ridge West."

Dawg was surprised. "Really? We didn't know that."

"Well, I believe it was registered to Mr Figgis's bank, but I know Mr Baxter paid something on it."

"How do you know this?" Dawg asked, although he probably knew.

"My fingers are still in the pie, Douglas," she said, mysteriously.

"You still have dealings with Mr Franklin's old company?"

"Indeed, Douglas. And they know *everything*." Martha's voice was almost trilling. "I am somewhat surprised that you and your colleagues, as law enforcers, are not more *au fait* with the situation, Douglas."

"Well," he stammered, "we know the bank holds several properties in the area, naturally. It's just that we hadn't quite put two and two together..."

"I am disappointed, Douglas. I would have thought Sheriff Withers was made of sterner stuff. But never mind."

Dawg tried to get himself on an even keel. "So, Mrs Franklin, what about Ralph Baxter and Copper Ridge West?"

"Well, as I said, I have read the newspaper this morning." She paused, waiting for a comment. There was silence. "It reported that poor Mr Baxter and the others died four days ago."

"That is correct."

"There have been people in the property since then, Douglas."

"Bank personnel, perhaps."

Martha sighed. "I think not. From my vantage point, I have a reasonable view of the place, and these three men do not look at all like the bank people that I know. One of them even appears to sleep out in the grounds at night."

Dawg thought she sounded shocked at that last revelation. "How do you know this?" he asked.

"I have seen it! How else would I know?"

Dawg repressed a gasp of fright. "You didn't recognise them, I suppose?"

"Too far away. My Marv designed these properties so that they all had very good privacy. It's just that our place is on the highest level, and my eyesight is still reasonably good. Otherwise, I might not have even noticed them."

Dawg wasn't sure that was true. Martha Franklin sees everything. Fortunately.

"I spoke with Raymond at the bank," she continued, "and he said he would look into it. I told him I would telephone you anyway, and he was not very happy with that idea, but I thought I would still let you know."

"I'm very grateful that you did, Mrs Franklin. Let me have the address, and we'll come out and take a look."

"Thank you, Douglas."

****

The drive up to Copper Ridge West was one of the most pleasant that Dawg had ever experienced. He'd never been in a position to even visit one of the properties on this complex, but he had seen photographs, especially the glossy ones. *Vanity Fair* had done a spread over several pages when some rap artist bought a bungalow up there, and even *Vogue* had taken some interior shots of a reality star's place. It was all beyond a deputy's meagre pay.

Withers sat beside him, reclining, as he always did, his hat on his lap and his eyes half-closed. Dawg knew he was wide awake, though.

Rafferty sat quietly in the back. He had insisted this time that Withers allowed him to come along for the ride, if only to appease his boss. There had been a marked silence for a while, but now Withers spoke.

"Okay, Pat, this here is what the locals call 'The Gotten Few'. The people with the money. The idle and not-so-idle rich."

"Nice area," commented Rafferty, as he stirred in his seat.

They were passing through the electronic gates at the entrance to the complex, after flashing their badges at the security guy. He didn't seem too concerned with their ID, probably accepting who they were because of the patrol car and the fact that two of them were in uniform. He did take a second look at the guy in the suit and the shades. Probably a banker gone rogue, he thought.

Dawg drove on until Withers called a halt. "We'll stop here, Dawg. A quiet arrival might be in order. Who knows what we might find?"

They parked under a two-hundred-year-old tree and got out. Dawg knew instinctively that his job was checking the rear of the property, so he made his way through the trees, unclipping the safety strap on his holster for reassurance. Withers looked at Rafferty, then started moving forward.

He kept up a steady pace, but the agent matched him, despite the limp. The path was winding, its route punctuated with colourful shrubs and miniature bushes. Not Baxter's work, Withers speculated. There was a woman's hand in this – presumably the previous owner.

They felt conspicuous as they approached the small lawn in front, as they could have been seen from the house for quite some time. Any prying eyes would be well aware of their presence.

Withers' radio crackled, Dawg confirming that he was in place. Withers stepped up to the door and rang the bell. They waited.

Dawg crouched behind what he thought was some kind of rhododendron, although he was no expert. It didn't smell, so there was no clue there. His eyes were trained on the back of the house. Nothing.

Withers rang the bell again, while Rafferty strained to look through one of the windows. They waited.

Dawg felt a twinge in his leg and had to change position. As he did so, he saw a shadow move in the house. He pinpointed a figure and rasped into his radio, "Boss, there's movement inside!"

After a second's pause, Withers responded, "Is he waving his arm in the air?"

Dawg studied the house. "Yes... how did you...?" He then realised that the figure inside was his sheriff.

"I'm not waving for fun, deputy. Get your ass in here now!" Withers ordered while smiling wickedly at Rafferty. Dawg mumbled, and was soon in with them, walking through an unlocked back door. "Front door was unlocked as well," Withers explained. "So, no breaking and entering." He looked at Rafferty. "I'm sure your boss would approve."

"I'm sure," Rafferty agreed. "But who gives a proverbial?"

"My sentiments exactly. Welcome to the team, Pat!" Withers grinned. They all laughed, although Dawg still felt a little nervous at being invited into the sheriff's innermost sanctum. He might get used to it... one day.

The house had clearly been occupied, but those responsible had gone in a hurry, leaving no physical trace.

"They knew we were coming, John," Rafferty said. "Did they see us?"

"Possibly," said Withers. "But they wouldn't have had time to clear everything out in the few minutes it took us to get up the drive. My guess is they've been tuning into our frequency, or they were given the nod."

Dawg said, "Mrs Franklin did speak with someone at the bank."

"Did she mention a name?"

"Raymond, she said."

Withers nodded. "Raymond Ross, the new bank supremo."

"Perhaps he sent someone up here," said Rafferty.

"Mm, it's a possibility. But I don't think so. We'll check with the security guy on the way out."

Rafferty pondered. "One thing, John, they couldn't have been using the gates at the entrance."

"No," said Withers. "They must have found a track somewhere and cut their way through the fence. I'll get somebody out there as soon as possible. Who knows, they may have even left a clue for us."

Rafferty grunted. "Ha! Would we be that lucky?"

The officers donned latex gloves and gave a cursory examination of each room, again with no success.

"It's down to forensics, I'm afraid," said Withers, pulling off his gloves as he stepped outside. "Let's hope they find something."

****

Number Two was frantic. He had expected to find a boat without difficulty. Instead, he was running

up and down the small harbour, waving his arms frantically and almost begging for help.

The General, seated in the shade of a small ketch pulled up onto the beach, watched with growing impatience. It shouldn't have been like this. His contact had told him it would all be so simple: go along with Leroy and just observe. When the shipment was unloaded back at Bakerton, he was to make a call, and someone else would arrange things from there on in. But how was he to know that Leroy had no intention of delivering the goods? It had been his intention all along to destroy a multi-million shipment of good-quality dope! Unbelievable. It made no sense whatsoever. The General studied the hills above the harbour, his nerves taut with expectation. He knew Lucas would be after them, somehow. It was only a matter of time. The General called to Number Two, "Double the offer!"

Number Two nodded and went on his way again, this time approaching an old salt-dog who was unravelling his fishing net. The two began an animated conversation, with both men pointing and shaking their heads in turn, as negotiations were conducted. Finally, Number Two came back to the General. "He wants more," he said.

"How much?"

"Three thousand."

"Okay," said the General. "Pay the man and let's get loaded."

As Number Two went to finalise the deal, the General knew that once at sea, he'd get his money back, and the salt-dog would take a swim.

****

The forensics officer-in-charge was Chad Orwell. He and Withers had worked together on a couple of minor incidents in the past, but this was the second time in a matter of days that Withers had called in on a serious case. They sat in Orwell's office, a sparsely filled room in the purpose-built Council Offices on Fitton Street. There had been talk of relocating the police station to these offices to save taxpayers' money, hence the opening of several law enforcement-related departments in the new building. The council, in its wisdom, had even incorporated holding cells and a small courtroom in the plans, but there had been a change of administration, and the idea fell into disrepute. Too late to stop forensics and the others from taking up residence, but it now meant that Withers had to commute between his old, crumbling station and this new, pristine edifice to man's folly.

Orwell greeted Withers and Rafferty warmly, shaking their hands and directing them to the seats around his desk. Withers took up the offer, while Rafferty, as usual, chose to hover in the background.

"Thanks for coming over, John. I appreciate this is always a culture shock for you." He chuckled at his own joke. Withers just grinned – the joke was *always* the same. Chad opened a large file. "We have evidence that two men were in the house over the last twenty-four hours. No prints, so they must have worn gloves at all times, but we found hairs."

"Good."

"We should get a match, but it will take time."

"Fair enough," Withers acceded. "But we had a report that there were three men. One apparently lived in the garden."

"We are checking the grounds now. As soon as something comes up, I'll let you know."

"Fine," said Withers. "And you're looking into the hole we found in the fence on the perimeter?"

Chad looked at his friend. "Was that an attempt at a joke, John?"

Sadly, it wasn't. "What did you make of the tyre marks and that sliver of paint we found on the fence out there?"

Chad said, "We're working on those. Looks like the vehicle drove into the fence to leave that patch of paint. We'll definitely get the manufacturer of the tyre, and the paint might well lead us to a make of car. It all takes time, I'm afraid."

Rafferty turned to face them. "Time we don't have," he said softly.

"So, what can we say about these men?" asked Withers.

"Not much until the hair is checked out, I'm afraid. I can tell you that they slept in separate rooms and that the second one appears to have a thing about big breasts."

They looked at him in awe. "How the hell do you know that?" asked Rafferty. "Forensics?"

Chad grinned. "Actually, yes. You know that big picture in the second bedroom?"

Rafferty knew it well because he had been searching that room, without success. "The lovely Salome," he said with a weak smile.

"That's the one." Chad waited, keeping his listeners enthralled. "Well, we found lip marks on one of her nipples."

"You mean...?" began Withers.

"Yes, when he went to bed, he must have been kissing her good night!"

DAY FIVE

Chapter Twenty

Brad Moody ran a very small logging business up on the top end of Copper Ridge, far away from the expensive properties in the area. A squat, muscular man who sported tattoos on both arms, it was hard to believe that he had sired the lovely Millie, the apple of his eye. Ex-navy, he had met his wife on a tropical island, and that was how their daughter got her stunning looks. Petal Moody had been killed six years ago when the car she was driving was struck by a falling tree in a particularly nasty gale. Most folk expected Brad to give up the lumbering business, but the irony seemed to have been lost on him, and he began to spend even more hours in the forest. Perhaps, in some bizarre way, it gave him comfort.

Now, he was in town, out of breath and striding towards the police station, ignoring the traffic and the people on the pavements, pushing past them in a haze. He saw nothing, felt only deep fear.

As he reached the door, he almost crashed into Dawg, who was coming out. Both men froze for a moment.

"Brad, you okay?" asked Dawg, seeing the other man's face. He didn't wait for a reply, instead guiding him into the station and on to a seat. He sat beside Brad and waited.

Brad took a deep breath. "It's my Millie…"

****

Withers sat opposite Brad Moody, his heart reaching out to his dear friend. He had rushed back to the office on receiving Dawg's urgent phone call, and he was now waiting for Brad to gather his thoughts. He appreciated that it wasn't easy, but they had to get the story about Millie as soon as possible.

Brad's breathing was fast and loud, his chest heaving with the exertion and the sheer panic he felt. He had run at full speed from his home a quarter of a mile away, slowing only to negotiate Bakerton's notorious main street, with its mix of vehicles and kamikaze pedestrians. Now, he was fighting to control his feelings of inadequacy over the disappearance of his daughter.

When he spoke, Withers' voice was soothing. "In your own time, Brad. We can go at your speed."

The words seemed to wake Brad up somehow, and he put his hand in the pocket of his overalls and brought out a card. "Millie phoned me the day before yesterday, from the diner…"

"Okay."

"She said she'd had a message from my sister Faith, asking her to call in. She said Faith was ill or something, so she was going over there." He paused. "I thought no more about it, although I was surprised she didn't let me know what was going on that night. I just assumed she was busy looking after April – that's Faith's daughter, my niece."

Withers nodded. "Youngster, is she?"

"Thirteen. Faith lost her husband some time ago. It's been tough for her."

"I bet," agreed Withers. "What's the card?"

Brad had been absent-mindedly playing with it, but now he handed it over. "I found it on my doormat this morning."

Withers read it aloud. "*Such a lovely little girl.*" He flipped the card and saw: LUCAS BLACK. Beneath the name was a fingerprint.

****

The truck ground to a halt. Lucas looked down at the harbour below, watching three men in camouflage fatigues and a couple of others hastily bundling packages into a small boat. He groaned, then drove on, hoping that he wasn't too late.

The road down from the hill was just as winding as all the others, the harbour disappearing from view for long seconds as Lucas navigated the terrain. He was racing as fast as he thought safe, although those in the back probably wouldn't have agreed with him. He shouted to Ralphie, "Get ready to shoot," and Baxter began to panic. He'd never fired a gun in his life before, and now was not the time to be practising. He swallowed hard and took up the weapon.

Although the locals grandly called it their harbour, in fact it was only a small bay, dotted with old boats and the occasional decrepit speedboat, now purely a decoration and a resting place for the gulls which came swooping down for fish entrails left by the departing fishermen. There was a pervasive smell of seaweed and decaying fish, unnoticed by the residents, but overpowering to the nostrils of the General.

As he turned away from the beach to gulp in some fresher air, he saw the old truck making its way dangerously down the hill. He realised at once who it was, and he knew it would be with them in less than five minutes.

"Number Two! Rifles! Quickly!"

The two other men in fatigues stopped loading and took up their weapons, running behind the boat for cover. The General stood in full view until the truck came to a stop, only then starting to retreat to a safe place.

Ralphie raised his rifle and aimed carefully, not sure how the weapon would react. Lucas was offering quiet instruction, but the adrenaline was pumping now, and Ralphie was ready. His finger gently eased the trigger back and then let it go, the whine of the bullet sounding so loud above the gentle swirl of the waves. Gulls took flight, and everyone on the beach froze, all eyes on the location of the shot. The only person who moved was the General, who stumbled, then fell face first onto the sand.

Ralphie gave out a whoop. "I don't bloody believe it!" he screamed, and Lucas had to agree with him. It was a fluke worthy of the name.

Lucas rallied his men. "Come on, let's get down there and finish them off."

The three of them ran across the beach, well fanned out, Ralphie and Nat yelling at the top of their voices, like a couple of banshees high on weed. Leroy, still in the truck, watched with growing trepidation, frightened for the safety of his men.

Number Two, reacting quicker than anybody else, had already dashed out and was hauling the wounded General into cover. Lucas raised his machine-gun and let off a burst, but it was pointless, because of the speed he was going and the unevenness of the shoreline, with its clumps of green and brown vegetation and the dips which held different levels of seawater. He watched as the bullets ricocheted harmlessly off the boats or scudded through the sand and plonked noisily into the water. The locals ran off in all directions, fearing for their lives. Lucas cursed his lack of control and told Nat and Ralphie to stop behind the nearest boat. They did so thankfully, each gasping for breath from the exertion and the fear coursing through them.

Lucas shouted, "General, you've got no chance. Give in now; otherwise we'll wipe you all off the face of the earth!" It sounded impressive, but Leroy would never let him carry out his threat. He knew it... and so, probably, did the General.

The General was in no fit state to reply. Number Two had propped him against the side of the boat and was putting a temporary dressing on his wound, using a piece of sail he had cut from the boat. The wound looked pretty bad, and he would need treatment fairly soon. The next few minutes were going to be critical. He ordered Number Three to start the dilapidated outboard motor and waited for it to roar throatily to life. And waited...

Chapter Twenty-One

Confirmation from the business card was swift. "Lucas Tyler Black," said Dawg, a certain excitement in his voice. "Although the fingerprint is slightly elongated due to the printing process, the tech boys are convinced it's his. He was born in Thornton, on 6th December 1976, son of Colin Peter Black and Maria Charlotte Cobden. Joined the Army in 1995 and served with distinction in a couple of theatres of war, most notably in Kosovo. Left the forces with an honourable discharge in February 2006, with some signs of battle fatigue, and then drifted for some time. He was off the radar until a minor traffic violation eight years ago. He was fined but was penniless at the time, so guess who picked up the tag?" He waited for Withers and Rafferty to play twenty questions. Instead, they just looked at him. He sighed, and said, "Leroy Figgis."

"So," said Withers, "they knew each other that long ago. What was the connection, I wonder?"

"Simple," Dawg replied. "Black's sister, Valerie, worked for Figgis at that time. I imagine Figgis helped him out, so he'd be owed one for the future."

"Good thinking," said Rafferty, inflating Dawg's ego just a bit. "Well done."

"Thank you, sir."

"So, where's the sister now?" asked Withers.

"Abroad somewhere – she's now an ambassador for one of Figgis's charities. Have suitcase will travel sort of thing."

"Okay, Dawg, she's not important," Withers decided. "But there is one thing for sure – Lucas Black didn't leave his own card."

"So, it must have been the General," added Rafferty.

Withers nodded. "He's been to a lot of trouble, having the card printed."

"Talk about a huge clue!" Dawg exclaimed.

Withers puffed out his cheeks. "The bastard wants *us* to track down Lucas for him!"

"Cheeky!" said Rafferty.

Dawg voiced his thoughts. "But how did he get the fingerprint? The tech guys said it must have come from Black's original army records or the police file. The quality is just too good to have been lifted from something Lucas might have touched."

"Friends in high places," offered Rafferty, and Withers had to agree.

Dawg let things drift for a moment, before saying, "Oh, and there's something else. Mr Orwell is in the outer office. He also has some news."

He slipped out and ushered the forensics man in. Withers greeted him warmly and waited.

"John, my boys have gone over the Ridge property with a fine-tooth comb. We've identified one of the men who stayed there."

"Better and better," chuckled Withers, sucking on another extra strong mint. They helped him concentrate.

"His name is Albert Dobson. Alby to his friends."

"Never heard of him," said Rafferty, and Withers nodded in agreement.

"Small-time crook out of Melton; that is, until he snapped and killed a guy with his bare hands in a bar-room quarrel. Spent ten years in Kinderville State Prison. Got out around a year ago and immediately went to ground. No sign of him since. The really interesting thing is, for much of his worthless life he was a fully-fledged hippy. He never saw a bed until he got locked up. He always slept in the open…"

"That's what Mrs Franklin said," interrupted Dawg. "She told me she thought one of them slept outside."

"And this is your guy. We found a bivouac round the side of the house. It was up a goddamn tree! There were beans cans and all sorts of other crap up there, all covered with his fingerprints. Careless, or what? But there's one more thing. During the early years of his incarceration, he got real friendly with another inmate who was inside for murder."

"Go on," urged Withers, sensing something special was just about to make an appearance.

Chad continued, "This guy – name of William Rhodes – was released from Kinderville just over four years ago. And," he added triumphantly, "he was inside for killing his old man with a single bullet between the eyes. Sound familiar?"

Withers whistled through his teeth. "Sure does, Chad. Let's find what we can about this William Rhodes. Get a picture sent over, and we'll see if Paul Cassidy ID's it. This guy might just be our General."

Chapter Twenty-Two

The moment I popped the old man, the world stopped. Sure, the old lady was scrambling to get off the bed, and her mouth was opening and closing like a big blubbery whale trying to get back into the water – but there was no sound. I knew she was screaming and shouting, but nothing was getting through to me. She got to the door, her nightdress hanging off her where she'd tried to jump me, one massive breast hanging down, and there she was, frantically trying to tuck it back out of sight. I might have laughed, but again there was no sound. I just felt my dry lips moving. The old man had crumpled over the side of the bed, blood draining from his wound. I reached down and stroked his forehead, some of the blood running through my fingers. He wasn't a bad father... just a dead one.

Sound suddenly came through in a rush. There were distant cries and a door slamming, the relentless tick of the clock on the bedside table. I stood up and walked into the living room, curled up in the armchair and switched on the TV using the remote. Some kind of kids' cartoon was playing. I smiled as the dog chased the cat and the cat chased the mouse, and the mouse frightened the woman of the house. It all seemed so normal.

I didn't hear the door open, but I sure felt the presence of Big Boris, our neighbour. Built like a brick outhouse, he stood in the doorway, waiting. I still had the gun in my hand, so I expect Boris was a bit nervous; but he needn't have been, because I would never hurt him. I liked Big Boris.

He came from Georgia. Not the US state, but the Soviet one. He'd been next door all my life, and we got on well, although he didn't like it much when I told people he was Russian. Apparently, the Georgians hate the Russians. What a mad world, eh?

He spoke to me, and I was surprised how gentle he sounded. It was as if the voice was coming from somebody else. He slowly walked over to me and put out his hand.

"C'mon, Billy, let me have the gun."

So, I let him have it!

Ha, I bet you thought I blasted him, didn't you? Well, I didn't. Like I said, I was fond of Boris. I handed him the gun and went back to my cartoon. It was way more interesting than real life.

Well, the upshot of my story is that Big Boris got a citation for bravery from the mayor… and I got to spend time in a youth institution, before being promoted to adult prison out in the desert somewhere. Life sucks, right?

I took to it pretty well, considering. I was tougher than most of the kids anyway, so the youth custody part was a *breeze. Most of them were shit-scared of me cos of what I'd done, so they kept their distance. And I kept mine.*

Prison – the real one, I mean – was different. I wasn't the big fish any more, so I had to play it cagey. I got in with a guy who liked boys, but I made it clear that I was off limits. I just had to find his playthings for him. No problem. The guys I was mixing with were just his type. Except for one. He was altogether a different can of worms by the name of Carl... Carl Ross. He was well spoken and had breeding, that was for sure. He lent me books and talked with me, man to man, so I spent a lot of time with him. He called me his protégé and said he was my mentor. Man, you didn't get those sorts of titles where I came from. He used to work for one of the big banks, but then had his 'little problem'. That's what he called it – his 'little problem'. Shit, it weren't so little! He had a fall-out with some of his dodgy investors and ended up carving up two of them in a back alley. He didn't give me the details, but I was mighty impressed anyway. Poppin' your old man doesn't compare, does it?

I spent three years of my sentence in the palm of Carl's hand, loving every minute and learning so much. Then it was all gone. Some punk did him in the shower, and I haven't been the same since. I never did find the guy who did for Carl, but I'm still looking...

It was a few weeks later that I started getting visits from Carl's little brother. Name of Ray...

Chapter Twenty-Three

Rafferty tossed the file onto Withers' desk with a flourish. "There you go, John, everything you ever wanted to know about William 'no middle name' Rhodes."

Withers looked up, impressed. "That was mighty quick," he beamed.

"Yep," said Rafferty. "They don't call me Quick-Draw McGraw for nothin'!"

"So, what have we got?" asked Withers, weighing the heavy folder in mid-air. "Feels like *War and Peace!*"

"Our boy has led a pretty interesting life, John. May I suggest you cancel your dinner-date with the enticing Ms Wiseman and instead curl up with the epic you hold in your hands?"

"Yes," agreed Withers, "you can suggest it. But you know what you can do with your suggestion."

"Noted. In your place, I would have said the same thing."

Withers grinned. "You'll never be in my place, Pat!"

The breakfast date had been a resounding success, and it hadn't taken Withers long to suggest dinner. Judith had accepted almost too eagerly, and they had shared a tender kiss on leaving Scotty's Diner. But it still left Withers in turmoil. Not only was he contemplating the replacement of Heather, but he also felt a real pang of guilt over the missing Millie. Surely he couldn't go out and enjoy himself while his friend's daughter was missing? Then again, he and his deputies, not to mention Rafferty and his agents, were doing everything they could to find her. Sitting at home, moping, was not going to help anyone.

He opened the file from Rafferty and revealed a glossy eight-by-twelve photograph of William Rhodes, taken on his release from prison. The authorities like to have a parting shot of their guests, just in case they feel like coming back any time soon. Next was a copy of his release paper, signed by the Governor and a few other dignitaries who had never seen the inside of an institution in their lives, but who, just possibly, ought to have done so on numerous occasions. Beneath that was a wad of paperwork which Withers had no inclination to wade through at this time. He closed the folder and put it to one side. "Anything *really* interesting in it?" he asked.

Rafferty shrugged. "Haven't read it all. My boys did all the donkey work. I'll probably read it tonight, after washing my hair. You know how it is when you've got nothing better to do."

"Can't say I do," grinned Withers.

"So, where are you taking the lovely lady?"

"I thought I'd go Mexican. What do you think?"

"Sounds good. There's nothing like spicing up an affair."

"Who said this is an affair?"

It was Rafferty's turn to grin. "And who said it isn't?"

****

El Encanto, Spanish for 'The Spell', was a small piece of Mexico on the through road to Thurlow Junction. Set back from the highway, it would be easy to miss, but its reputation meant that most of its clientele were returning gourmands and aficionados of real Spanish and Latin American food.

An extremely nervous Withers had picked Judith up outside her hotel, and she had enjoyed the open-top drive in the cool evening air, listening to Django and watching Withers tap out the rhythm on the steering wheel.

"Do you play anything?" she had asked.

"Chess."

"No," she had said, laughing, "I meant music. Guitar? Drums?"

"Neither."

"Does that mean 'nothing'?"

"Yes," he had told her, "nothing." Then he had said, "Nobody will ever play music as well as the maestro. So why bother trying?"

"That is a very negative attitude, if you don't mind me saying."

"I don't."

The track had changed to *Dream of You*, and Withers had been once more transported. "You know," he had explained, "Django was injured in an accident. He had to learn a completely new way of playing the guitar. So, as I said, it would be impossible to reproduce his virtuosity."

As they had turned into the restaurant car park, she had glanced at her companion and smiled. This was going to be a wonderful evening.

They were now sat at their table, close to the large bay-fronted window, where they could look out onto the rolling hills and the distant motorway. Not exactly a prime view, but it was enough for Judith, and Withers only had eyes for her anyway.

"Do you come here often?" she asked, with a twinkle in her eye.

"I bet that's what you say to all the guys."

"Perhaps I should have said it in Spanish."

He grinned. "Ha, you'd end up dating every waiter in the place."

"Not the way my Spanish goes!" she said with a wink.

The waiter brought the menus and wine list, and Withers made a show of studying the latter like a professional, before ordering the house white. The waiter took the order with a straight face and went away.

"I read your article," Withers said, eventually. "On Figgis."

She smiled. "What did you think?"

"Very good." He paused. "I also read the one you did on him last year."

The waiter returned with the wine and, with a Latin flourish, pulled the cork and poured a taster, which Withers dismissed with a wave of his hand, and the waiter filled their glasses, Judith's first, before disappearing once again. She took a sip and studied the sheriff. "Well, what did you think?" His face was passive, neutral, so she could not read him, as she could with most other men. To her, he was an enigma wrapped up in a comfortable suit, but clearly more at home in his sheriff's uniform.

"He sounded a very nice chap, as the English might say."

"He was." Judith was sincere; Withers saw it in her eyes. "He was old-world polite – you know, calling me ma'am – and the respect was obvious. He didn't look down on me as a second-class citizen."

"Even though you were just a journalist," Withers teased.

"*Just* a journalist?" she said with mock-indignation, and they both laughed. "He did a lot of good, John. He had his own foundation for kids and promoted several other charities. He was one of life's good guys." She took another sip of wine.

"So, it might surprise you to learn that he was a drug runner," he said, out of the blue.

Judith almost choked on her drink. "What?"

Before the conversation could continue, the waiter appeared to take their order. He saw the lady was a little flustered, so he kept his eyes on the big man sitting opposite her. "Will you order now, *señor*?"

Withers looked at Judith. "What are you eating?"

She struggled to speak. "I haven't had time to think about it."

The waiter seized the moment. "May I suggest the house's *Hot Tamale*," he said with almost a leer. "It is a dish of meats and cheeses steamed in corn husks. *Exquisito!*"

Judith and Withers agreed at once, pleased that they didn't have to make the decision. As the waiter left, he said over his shoulder, "Of course, the name also means 'sexual attractiveness', *señorita*. I am sure you will enjoy!"

Judith almost blushed. Withers couldn't hold back a chuckle. "I said you'd end up with all the waiters! So, there's the first."

"John!" she blurted, her hand over her mouth. "Stop it!"

They settled back, an easy silence descending. Finally, she said, "Are you serious?"

"About Figgis?" She nodded, so he continued, "Yes, I am. I have irrefutable proof. I'm sorry to burst your bubble."

"I still can't believe it." She took a sip of her wine to hide her confusion. "I researched everything. There wasn't a whiff of scandal or illegal dealings about him."

"We've checked him out," said Withers. "We also came up blank. He must have covered his tracks pretty well. All we could find were a few dodgy dealings in diamonds; but, again, nothing concrete. We can only assume that the last drug run went terribly wrong. That's why he was murdered."

"Why have you told me this, John?" she asked warily. "Obviously I can't publish."

"Obviously not!" he responded, looking into her eyes. "I told you because… because I felt it was right. I didn't do it to upset you or prove a macho point. I want your input."

Judith sat back. "Really? Well, I say again: I don't believe it. What proof do you have?"

"His contact on Lanscarges."

Judith's face dropped. "Seriously?"

"Yes. He arranged two pick-ups for Figgis four years ago..."

"Hold on, four years ago? So why was he only murdered now, all this time later?"

"We don't know. That's another thing we're working on."

"But you're convinced the two incidents are connected."

Withers said, "Pretty much so. The only clues we have all lead us to that conclusion."

The waiter brought over their food and winked at Judith, before retreating to a safe distance, where he kept his eye on the couple. He felt the vibes coming off the table and wondered whether something romantic might be happening. Withers was hoping the same but had no real confidence, so he tucked into his meal, the meat and melted cheese smelling wonderful as it oozed over the corn husk.

With no preamble, Judith suddenly said, "Tell me about Heather."

Withers stopped, mid-fork. "What?"

"I'd like to know all about her."

"Why?"

"Because I need to know more about you – and she *is* you, isn't she?"

Withers put his fork down, the food untouched, and looked at Judith. "I don't talk about her."

"Well, you should. She was your life, John."

He really didn't know what to say. Heather had been gilt-wrapped into a little parcel and placed on a shelf in his heart, never to be touched again. And now here was a woman asking if he would open that parcel and expose everything – the love, the hurt… the hate. "No," he said eventually, "Heather is gone."

Judith knew that wasn't true, but again it was too early in their relationship to pursue it, so she placed her hand on his and said, "I understand. So let's just enjoy the evening, and indulge in this 'sexual attractiveness', shall we?"

He smiled weakly and thought of Heather.

****

When he got home, Withers did not feel at all tired. He poured himself a whisky and water, threw off his shoes, and stepped into the lounge. It had been a good evening, despite Judith wanting to talk about things that didn't concern her. Or perhaps they did? What did he feel about her? She was attractive, yes; sexy, yes; intelligent, yes. Great company, without question. What was there not to like?

He sank into the sofa and took a long slug of the drink, feeling the watered-down whisky hitting the spot like it always did. A bad day at the office always led to this ritual, and it seemed to be happening more often than not these days.

His eye strayed to the table, where he had earlier placed the folder from Rafferty. Oh, well, he thought, let's have a look. A bit of night-time reading. He placed his tumbler on the coffee table, slid off the sofa and picked up the folder. There was so much in it that he decided to sit at the table. He opened the folder, seeing once again the glossy photo of William Rhodes. He spent a minute studying the man's features, trying to get into his mind. He had received confirmation earlier, before his dinner date, after Paul Cassidy had made a formal ID. Withers knew without question now that he was looking at the General. He couldn't hold back a shiver.

He settled down to study the contents, sheet by sheet. Much of it was of no interest to him, so he offered only a cursory look at them. There was the birth certificate, of course; doctors' records from several decades... Hold on a minute! Pandando said that the General had been *wounded*!

With a renewed vigour, Withers went through the medical records, looking for something within the last four years to indicate that a procedure had been carried out. He found nothing, and banged his fist on the table in frustration. He gulped down the remains of his drink and went to the kitchen for a refill.

Next were Rhodes' bank details. Everything appeared to be pretty straightforward. But something stood out: he had received two considerable lump sums. One was around four years ago, and the other only last year, both from what looked to be the same unknown source. That wasn't an insurmountable problem – Pat Rafferty would track down the person responsible.

As Withers worked his way through the paperwork before him, he refilled his glass two more times, sipping in between studying. He was getting towards the end, and feeling suddenly so tired, when he found something else. Wrapped in a frayed rubber band was a small pile of green pieces of paper. Withers knew what they were at once and, intrigued, he took off the band and flattened out the sheets. They were carbon copies of Prison Visit forms…

****

Lucas and the others were getting closer. They had spread out and were beginning to close in on the General and his men. Now their only exit was by sea.

Number Two picked up the General and placed him as carefully as he could into the boat. Two fishermen who had been loading the packages threw a tarpaulin over him and took up station ready to set sail. It was a long shot, but there was no alternative.

There was a prolonged burst of machine-gun fire from Nat, who had no idea how the thing worked, but at least it kept everyone on their toes. Lucas joined in, while Ralphie, now the sharpshooter, revelled in the idea of peppering the boat with bullets. It was all furious but futile, and the boat with the General slowly moved out to sea.

It was then that one of those quirks of fate took hold of the situation and threw it completely off balance. Number Three raised his head to get a shot at Lucas. A volley from Nat somehow thundered into the boat, again more by luck than judgement, and ripped through Number Three, peeling off skin and cartilage, bone and sinew, and a fair proportion of his face and brain. He fell back into the boat – and gave Number Two the answer to his prayers.

Moving swiftly, he removed the distinctive ring from the General's finger and placed it on the same finger of Number Three. It wasn't a perfect fit, but Number Two hoped that Lucas, in his moment of triumph, would overlook that. He also put the

General's pistol into the dead man's pocket, ensuring that the grip was visible. He knew that the others were well aware of the General's prize possession.

Number Two then carefully placed the body overboard and prayed that it would float in on the tide, and not out to sea.

The water turned crimson as the body bobbed on the water. For interminable seconds, it looked as if it would be sucked out to the deep, but Number Two gave a silent prayer as it began to make its slow way towards the beach.

The boat was well out to sea by the time Lucas reached the edge of the surf, but all he could think about was the body, which had come to rest face-down at the water's edge. He stopped, his brow furrowed and sweating, and he knew it was about to happen again. He could hear gunfire in the distance, and now there was the unmistakeable roar and whizz of incendiary devices and sniper shots, as well as the screams and horror-sounds of a pitched battle. His eyes were clouding over, and his heart rate seemed to him to have doubled. He crouched, machine-gun at the ready, his eyes attempting to focus and look around for the unseen enemy. Now he could see a small sailboat bobbing on the water, but it was harmless – just some poor local fishermen caught up in the mêlée of battle. He waved frantically at them, trying to make them get away quickly before the enemy swarmed in and killed them all. It was about to be a bloodbath, and he, too, wanted to flee, but his training was kicking in, and he lay prone on the sand, awaiting orders from his CO.

Nat and Ralphie stopped in their tracks and ceased their firing, stunned by the actions of their leader. They looked at each other, bewildered, and Nat shouted, "Lucas, are you okay?"

Lucas heard the command, "Lucas, win the day!" and he responded by getting to his feet and charging into the sea, leaving his machine-gun on the sand. The sound of the battle was getting more intense, and he had to do something. There was a body in the water – the enemy – and he lunged for the pistol in the corpse's combat jacket pocket.

Without thinking, he rubbed a hand over the scar on his neck and was consumed with hatred. He examined the pistol, hoping the mechanism hadn't been flooded, and before Nat or Ralphie could catch up with him, he put two bullets into the back of the body and tossed the gun and the ring from the dead man's finger far out to sea.

As he tumbled into the surf, the sounds of battle left his head, and he began to cry...

Chapter Twenty-Four

Number Three was not comfortable. He didn't like long spells inside, away from healthy air and the sounds of the birds. It was too much like prison.

The only thing that made it all worthwhile was the blonde missy lying in front of him. The General had told him to tie her up, but Alby didn't like that idea. The same as he didn't like being called Number Three. He'd been a number inside, so he sure as hell didn't want that now. Alby was his name, and that's what he was going to use.

It had been exciting to begin with. Billy had been waiting for him when he got out of prison, and took him off to a smart motel, laying on beer and sausage rolls, his favourite. He'd been so grateful that he didn't object when Billy dubbed him Number Three, after some foreign guy who had apparently laid down his life for Billy. No names, he'd said, for what we are about to do. Okay, Alby had replied, a face full of roll. Who cares? I'm out of the slammer!

But it was different now. Alby had fulfilled his obligation. He'd been there when Billy got his revenge on Figgis, and that was the end of it. He looked at the girl on the bed. She was just beginning to stir, and he was pleased. He would like to talk to her.

"Good morning," he said breezily.

Millie coughed and tried to sit up. Alby was at her side immediately, gently holding her down. "Take it easy, Millie. Let the chloroform wear off a bit more."

Chloroform? Millie's head was spinning for all sorts of reasons. Where was she? How did she get here? She tried to focus her eyes. She saw a small room, furnished with the bed she was on, an armchair and a bedside cabinet, all looking pretty dingy and dank. A short, stocky man stood by the closed door, and he was smiling at her. Smiling!

"Who are you?" she asked, blinking as her eyes began to grow accustomed to the dim light coming in from the very small window above her. "Where am I?"

Alby carried on smiling. He really liked the look of this girl. *So* pretty. "I'm Alby," he said, as if that fact alone would reassure the girl. He took a step forward, and she recoiled in horror. Alby stopped and raised his arms. "I'm not gonna hurt you. Honest."

Millie looked into his eyes and saw nothing but the loving gaze of a man-child. She gathered strength from the fact. "Okay, Alby," she said gently, "where are we?"

"Oh, I can't tell you that!" he replied, the smile getting wider, if that was possible. "It would spoil the game."

"Game?"

"Billy said it was a game, see. I had to pick you up and keep you here, and he would come back later to let you go."

Millie digested things; and at once she knew a stark fact: when this Billy came back, he would kill her. There was no two ways about it, and she had to find a solution. She forced a smile. "Let me get this straight, Alby. You used chloroform to kidnap me..."

"No!" he pleaded. "No, I didn't kidnap you. I wouldn't do something like that to a pretty girl like you. Billy asked me to bring you here, so I did." He looked proud of the fact he had carried out his instructions, but a frown creased his brow. "Mind, I didn't do everything Billy said."

"What else was there?" asked Millie, nervously.

Alby looked sheepish. "He told me to tie you up. But I couldn't do that, could I? Not a pretty girl like you."

Millie wasn't keen on the way he kept describing her as pretty, wondering whether he might just take things a little further. She sat up. "I'm mighty glad you didn't tie me up. Thanks."

230

He nodded happily. "No thanks needed," he said. "I like you."

That thought alone sent shivers down her spine, and she knew even more that she had to get outside, wherever she was. "Listen, Alby, can I go to the bathroom?" It was an old ploy, but it always worked in the movies. Perhaps she could squeeze out through the bathroom window and make a run for it.

"Sure," Alby said, opening the door and pointing to another door to the right, it's peeling paint offering no chance of a pristine bathroom beyond. Millie saw another door straight ahead and assumed it was the front door. No hope there, she thought; even Alby wouldn't be stupid enough to let her get to it and taste freedom.

She made her way unsteadily out of the bedroom and turned the knob on the door to the bathroom. She wished she hadn't. It wasn't just the smell. The walls were caked in a nasty shade of grunge, and the small sink was cracked in several places, while a mirror above it looked as if it might have considerably more than seven years' bad luck. The toilet had no seat and bore the indelible markings of a hundred previous users. To cap it all, there was no window.

"On second thoughts," she said, "I don't need to go."

"Sorry, Millie. What do you expect from an old farmhouse, miles from anywhere?"

That last comment deflated her, and she dejectedly traipsed back to the bedroom and threw herself onto the bed, almost resigning herself to her fate. She was never going to get out of this…

****

The lake looked tranquil and peaceful, so the General sat at its edge and just stared. Number Two was thirty yards away, behind a tree, keeping watch. He played with the pistol in his pocket, looking forward to the next time he could draw it in anger.

The General had fond memories of a similar lake, but not so big and blue. His lake had a canoe, and he would spend hours as a boy, paddling around, keeping a distance both physically and mentally between himself and his parents. There, he could be what he wanted and do what he liked. He would stop the canoe in the centre of the lake and just stroke the surface of the water, feeling the droplets between his fingers. A bit like his father's blood…

He came back to the present with a start and shivered. Number Three was looking after the girl, so it was now time to set the ball in motion. He removed from his backpack one of two on-the-go mobile phones he had bought earlier. He dialled a number, and a female voice said, *"Altona Oracle* office. How may I help?"

The General was impressed with the girl's efficiency. He just hoped she would continue to show such control as the conversation developed. "I'd like to speak to Judith Wiseman," he said sharply.

"I'm sorry, sir, but Judith is busy at the moment. May I get her to pho…?"

"Listen!" he said with venom. "You have thirty seconds to get her on the phone – or I will kill the girl."

"What?" screamed the telephonist.

"I will start counting… now!"

It was twenty-four seconds later that Judith gripped the telephone with sweaty palms. "Who is this?"

"Ah, Ms Wiseman, I presume? I have a little favour to ask of you."

Judith was shaking. "Who are you?"

"They call me the General."

"Never heard of you. You could be any old sicko trying to make a name for yourself," she responded.

"Indeed, I could be. But I am the real McCoy, Judith. I *am* the General. And I can prove it. Now listen to me. I will give you ten minutes to talk to your friend Sheriff John Withers. You will tell him that Figgis was killed with a Glock 17 – got that, a Glock 17. This is not public knowledge, as you well know, so when he confirms it, you will know who you are dealing with. Then you can do me that favour."

The General hung up and tossed the phone as far as he could into the lake. He then got up, brushed down his trousers and returned, whistling, to the car, Number Two shadowing him all the way.

****

Precisely ten minutes later, the General used the second phone to call the *Oracle* office. Number Two had driven the car one mile around the lake and parked up in the nature trail car park, as far away as he could from the log cabin information centre manned by a couple of lake rangers, in their Lincoln green uniforms. A class of schoolchildren had just enjoyed a dip in the lake and were congregating around the cabin, their teacher acting like a mother hen, cajoling them into some semblance of order before they were led into the building and out through the other side into the wilds of the forest.

The General had walked in amongst some trees by the water's edge. He was ready when somebody answered.

"Is that you, General?" said Judith, who had been hovering over the phone since she had received confirmation from Sheriff Withers on the firearm used in the massacre. She had networked the phone line, so Withers could listen in from his office in Bakerton.

"Miss Wiseman. How pleasant to hear your voice again. I take it that you are convinced of my authenticity? And I assume Sheriff Withers is privy to this conversation?"

Withers cursed mentally but said nothing.

Judith said, "Where is the girl, and what do you want?"

"One thing I do not want is the girl, Miss Wiseman. You can have her if you give me Lucas Black."

"I don't know a Lucas Black..."

"Perhaps not, but the sheriff does, don't you, Mr Withers?"

"What do you have in mind?" Withers' voice was rasping, on edge. "You know we don't have Black. You know our every move."

"True," said the General, "so that's why I'm asking for Ms Wiseman's help."

"What do you want me to do?" asked Judith, frightful of the answer.

"It's so simple, my dear. I want you to publish something in your newspaper. It will be in code, so only Black will understand the meaning. You can do that little thing for me, can't you?"

"What about the girl?" burst in Withers.

"Like I said, you will get her when I have Black in my hands."

"And you will kill him," said Withers with no feeling.

"Oh, yes, I most certainly will," laughed the General as he hung up.

Following the abrupt ending of the call, it took a moment for Judith to get her voice back. "John, what are we going to do?"

Withers tried to soothe her. "It's okay, Judith. The General will be sending you something in the near future, I'm sure. Send it over to me, and I'll get a team of codebreakers on standby. Just make sure your editor prints it."

****

After throwing the phone into the lake, just like the last one, the General made his way back to the car, where Number Two wound down the driver's window. He had a laptop on the passenger seat beside him.

"Send it," said the General. "Our love letter to Lucas Black!"

Chapter Twenty-Five

It didn't take long for Withers and Rafferty to receive the email from Judith. Withers sat in front of the laptop, while Rafferty looked over his shoulder.

"I think you can forget the codebreakers," advised Rafferty.

Withers nodded. "Yes, there's no way anyone can work this out."

They studied the text for the fourth or fifth time.

A MESSAGE FOR LUCAS BLACK

Hi, comrade! Long time no see. Hey, I've picked up a nice little package that some people are worried about. Can you guess what it is? Well, it's up to you to make sure it's returned to its loved ones. All you've got to do is come see me, and I'll send back the package, complete with a big red bow if you like. Sound good?

I've been studying the Bakerton street map, and you'll never guess what! Remember the old haunt that P and C used to hang out in? Well, they've got one right here in town. Fancy that!

All you've got to do is meet me there on Friday at noon. I like noon, Lucas. It's just like that old western.

Make sure you come with empty pockets. I don't want to damage the package, do I?

The General

"Cocky little scumbag, isn't he?" commented Rafferty bitterly. "So, what do you make of it?"

Withers looked up at him. "Well, it's pretty clear who the package is."

"Millie Moody."

"But where did Piers and Cameron used to meet up?"

Rafferty squinted, as he always did when he was thinking. "You're sure it's Cameron?"

"The P is surely Piers Fleming. He was always known as P."

"Yes," agreed Rafferty, "but shouldn't 'C' be an 'N' if we're talking about Nat Cameron?"

"I don't know, Pat. Who does know how these guys think?" Withers re-read the text yet again. "It just doesn't make sense."

Rafferty stepped away. "I'm sure it will, to Lucas Black."

"Yes," agreed Withers, "but only if he sees it. And we have no way of guaranteeing that."

Rafferty sighed. "We don't even know if he can read!"

"Don't be unkind, Pat! Remember, he was in the military – they don't take just anybody, you know."

"So," said Rafferty, "we need to give this blanket coverage. I can arrange regular announcements over the radio."

"I knew you'd come in handy some time," laughed Withers.

"What, so the coffee and cake runs don't count?"

Withers suddenly got serious. "Millie Moody's life is at stake here, Pat, so we need to cover all bases. You sort out the radio stations, and I'll get my men to put pressure on the shopkeepers to put signs in their windows. We must get through to Lucas Black somehow."

Chapter Twenty-Six

It was late in the afternoon, and the newsagent was putting a poster in his A-frame as Ty walked by. He thought that was an odd thing to be doing, so he stopped and watched, assuming that there was some breaking news which warranted extra coverage. He began chatting to the man and asking him if there was anything interesting happening.

The man shook his head. "Not a lot. We've just been asked to put these posters up by the police. Something to do with the Figgis killings, so they say." He finished fixing the poster and stepped back, wiping a tuft of his grey, wavy hair out of his eyes. "Strange business, if you ask me."

"Sure is," Ty said, but he had already read the poster, and his mind was racing. It told him that he, Lucas Black, *must* get a copy of tomorrow's *Altona Oracle*. It was a matter of life and death. As he walked away, waving to the newsagent, he was churning things over in his mind. What the hell was going on? The cops obviously knew who he was now, but why should he have to buy a copy of the local rag? It made no sense, but he had to go along with it. He knew only that it would lead him to the Arsehole.

****

The food was pretty good, to be fair, and Millie tucked in as if it were her last meal. That sobering thought was no match for the hunger she felt, and the rabbit stew went down a treat, even though she wasn't too sure about the protein element. Perhaps it would have been better if Alby hadn't told her what it was. But she knew that, whatever the outcome, she had to keep up her strength.

Alby unlocked the door. "Everything okay for you?" he asked, desperate for positive feedback.

"Scrumptious," said Millie, in between mouthfuls.

He silently mouthed the word, a wide grin breaking out on his face. "That's a lovely word, Millie," he said. "Scrumptious."

Millie watched him intently. She had been here, what, two days, perhaps? To be honest, she had no idea of the time, or even what day it was. Alby – or someone – had taken her watch. All she did know with any certainty was that Alby, for all his faults, was never going to hurt her. So, she reasoned, why not just get up and walk out? Ask him nicely for the key, step outside, and walk for as long as it takes to find sanctuary; a truck on the road, perhaps, or an inhabited farmhouse just across a field. She studied Alby's face. His smile was warm, and his eyes sparkled, and he seemed to hop slightly from one leg to the other, just like an excited toddler. Surely, she can get through to him.

"A walk would be nice," she ventured.

"Oh, yes!" agreed Alby. "I'd like that." Then his smile wavered as his brain took over. "But Billy wouldn't like it."

"I wouldn't tell him," said Millie. "It would be our secret. Just a quick stroll outside, in the fresh air. You could hold my hand, if you wanted."

Oh, he would dearly love that! He could show her his camp out in the woods, his life beyond man-made walls. He was so tempted.

Just then…

His cell phone erupted into 'Let It Go' from *Frozen*, and he jumped back to reality. He put the phone to his ear. "Hello?" Pause. "Oh, hello, Billy… sorry, General. Yes, she's fine. Just having lunch. I cooked rab… Sorry, right, okay. Whatever you say."

Millie's moment had gone.

Chapter Twenty-Seven

Withers had passed on the bank details to Rafferty, but he knew who was responsible. The Prison Visit forms had told him that.

This time when he entered the Mercurial Bank, it was business as usual. There was no vestige of the pain and anguish shrouding the staff last time. Now, they were once again an efficient and professional workforce, helping you to handle your money and creaming off a goodly percentage at the same time. The world was back on its axis.

He went straight to the lift and punched in the required floor. He didn't even bother with an extra strong mint. He was wound up too much for luxuries like that. The lift stopped with the bodyless man's voice thanking him for taking the ride, and Withers stepped out and strode towards the office he required.

"Excuse me!" a woman's voice echoed through the corridor. Withers ignored her. "You need to go through me, sir!" she pleaded, her tone getting higher with each word. "Sir, sir!"

Withers burst through the office door and stopped. Raymond Ross had been in deep conversation with a thin, weedy looking man, but they both froze, mouths agape.

"I suggest you invest your money elsewhere, sir," Withers said. "Good day to you."

The weedy man looked at Withers, then to Ross, then back to Withers. "I..."

Withers made a show of offering him the door. "Good day, sir!" he shouted much more forcefully, and the man scurried out, mumbling something about the quality of some banks. Tell me about it, thought Withers.

Ross finally found his voice. "What the hell is going on, sheriff?" he demanded, hoping he sounded authoritative, although not exactly feeling it.

"Mr Ross," said Withers slowly, "we need to talk."

At that moment, the receptionist hurried into the room. "I'm so sorry, Mr Ross, he just..."

Withers said, "William Rhodes," and saw at once that Ross was on the defensive.

"Thank you, Margery. It's absolutely fine. The sheriff has an appointment."

"Not in my book," she replied indignantly.

"Sorry, my fault," Ross placated her, and she pulled back, closing the door behind her. Ross tried to control his breathing. "Now, sheriff, what can I do for you?"

Withers moved to the desk and stood over it, casting a large shadow over the seated man. "You know William Rhodes."

"Er, yes, yes, I do. Why? What has he done?"

"You tell me, Mr Ross."

"I don't understand."

"You gave Mr Rhodes two large sums of money." Withers hadn't received confirmation from Rafferty yet, but he just *knew*.

There was no sense in denying it. "Yes, I did. So?"

"Do you mind if I ask you what they were for?"

"Yes, I do mind," countered Ross, wondering how much the lawman actually knew.

Withers eased back on the pressure. "Perhaps you could tell me how you know William Rhodes."

Ross wasn't stupid. "I'm sure you know, sheriff."

"I'd like you to tell me."

"Very well." Ross opened a drawer and took out a hip flask. "Drink?" Withers shook his head, so Ross found a glass in the drawer and poured out a large tot. He took a swig. "He was an acquaintance of my brother, Carl."

"Go on," said Withers. He hadn't had time to track down all the details, so he was flying by the seat of his pants, not an unusual position to find himself in. He needed Ross to fill in the gaps.

"Carl was a banker, like myself. One day, he got into a little fracas and ended up in prison. He met and befriended Billy there."

"Billy."

"Yes. That's the name I knew him by."

"So how did you meet Billy?"

To Withers' surprise, Ross took a deep gulp and suddenly looked a frail and beaten man. The change in him was so dramatic that Withers felt the shockwaves pass through him.

"Carl was… murdered in prison, sheriff." Ross stopped, choked. "Murdered," he repeated.

"I'm sorry," said Withers truthfully.

"I started to visit Billy shortly after. Carl had spoken highly of him, so I thought the least I could do was meet him."

"A killer," said Withers with contempt.

"Yes, but I thought he could help me."

Withers understood. "To find Carl's killer."

"That was the plan, yes. But it never happened."

"So why maintain the connection with Rhodes?" asked Withers.

"For old times' sake, I suppose," said Ross.

"So what about the money you gave him?"

"They were just loans."

"Or payment for a job to be done," said Withers pointedly.

"What do you mean?"

"The murder of Leroy Figgis, perhaps."

"That's absurd!" blurted Ross, reaching for his glass and polishing off the contents. "If you intend to make insinuations, sheriff, then I must insist on having my lawyer present."

"Of course you do, Mr Ross," said Withers. "But that will be all for now. No doubt I will be in touch again shortly." He went to the door, opened it and stopped. "Please don't think about leaving the country, sir. Even if you do now have access to Mr Figgis's private jet." He had yet another parting shot. "When you see the General again, Mr Ross, tell him I'm getting closer." And then he was gone.

Raymond Ross was shaking with anger and something else, something he had never really experienced before... fear. He reached for his hip flask again, but before he could take a medicinal gargle, the door opened. The bulk of Sheriff Withers filled the doorframe, and Ross gulped and bit his top lip at whatever onslaught was about to overcome him. Whatever he had expected, it wasn't what Withers delivered.

"Oh, and another thing, Mr Ross. We've had the post-mortem on Leroy Figgis..."

Ross waited, paralysed.

"He had a particularly virulent form of cancer."

"I didn't know that," said Ross weakly.

"He would have been dead within a few weeks." Withers paused. "There wasn't really much point in killing him, was there?"

Ross was a wreck. He couldn't understand how everything was unravelling before his very eyes. Even if the sheriff didn't know now, he would soon find out that the first sum of money had been used for medical treatment overseas. Getting a bullet safely out of someone's back is not a cheap affair, and the surgeon he hired came with so many add-ons that the costs escalated alarmingly. He had demanded six of the finest nurses, an eminent anaesthetist, an operating theatre sister of impeccable credentials – and then he'd demanded another ten thousand for keeping quiet. Ross didn't know why he hadn't just put a bullet in the General. It would have been considerably cheaper.

He poured another large glassful of drink and downed it in one go. His head was beginning to feel fuzzy, but it was also becoming crystal clear that this couldn't go on much longer.

DAY SIX

Chapter Twenty-Eight

Ty was on the street before the newspapers hit. He went to a different newsagent for his copy, then picked up a coffee-to-go, and went.

Once back in his flat, he opened the paper and began to scan it. It didn't take long. He saw his name on page three, and he read through the message between sips of the warm but flavourless drink. So, they were getting close to the showdown they both wanted.

He re-read the piece and put the paper down. He was confused by this 'package' the General had referred to. Surely it couldn't be some of the dope from Lanscarges... that had been seized by the local coastguards after Leroy had put out the alert. True, Number Two had obviously bailed out some time before the boat's capture and had presumably high-tailed it into the woods; but Ty and Leroy had been assured that all the drugs had been taken into custody, along with two very bewildered and scared Spanish fishermen, together with their loud-mouthed skipper, who complained bitterly that the

General and his associate had stolen his three thousand notes. Ty had assumed that Number Two was now living off this small sum in isolation somewhere.

It was only then that everything finally clicked into place. Since Leroy's death, he had accepted that the Arsehole had tricked him. The body in the water had clearly been a nobody, and Number Two had spirited the General away before his very eyes. He cursed out loud at his stupidity. But, of course, Number Two must have come over with the General to wreak havoc on poor Leroy and the others. It made so much sense that he couldn't believe he'd missed it.

But what about this package? It must be important because the General was using it as a bargaining chip. He needed to know what he was up against, and there was only one person to ask...

****

"Sheriff Withers?"

"No, this is Special Agent Rafferty. The sheriff is out of the office."

"I need to speak to him – urgently."

"In what connection, may I ask?"

"Leroy Figgis."

Rafferty clutched the phone a little tighter. "Go on."

"I'll only speak to Withers."

"Okay, give me your number, and I'll get him to call you."

"Can't do that."

"Really? Why not?"

"Security."

"What kind of security?"

"Mine."

Rafferty had been edging to the door, and finally managed to get his hand on the knob. He opened the door and gestured to Deputy Lenier, who sprang out of his chair. Rafferty cupped his hand over the mouthpiece and mimed to the deputy that he should get hold of Withers pretty damn quick. Lenier went out, and Rafferty moved back into the office.

"Are you still there?" said the voice.

"Yes, sorry. Can you give me your name?"

"Only to Withers."

"He's on his way. Can you hold?"

"What, and let you trace me? No chance." He hung up just as Withers raced into the office.

"What is it, Pat? Can't a man have a crap break, for God's sake? I thought Phil was going to smash down the door."

The phone rang again. Withers indicated that Rafferty should answer it.

"It's me again."

"Good," soothed Rafferty.

"I'll talk to you, Agent Rafferty. This can't wait."

"Okay. What's on your mind?"

"I'm Lucas Black."

Rafferty slid into the sheriff's chair, his face awash with surprise and concern. "Mr Black."

Withers winced and sat on the edge of the desk, listening in. He didn't want to put the caller off, so he decided to let Rafferty carry on.

"I've got a copy of the paper."

"We're so pleased," breathed Rafferty, the relief clear in his voice.

Ty picked up on it. "So, this is important to you as well as me."

"Yes, it is."

There was a pause. "So what's this package the Arsehole refers to?"

Both Withers and Rafferty smiled despite themselves. If only they had thought of that name for the killer.

Rafferty bit his lip. "We need your help, Mr Black."

"Really? Well, that's rich, I must say. Explain."

"This is very serious, Mr Black," said Rafferty. "Please be clear on that."

"Okay. I can do serious."

It was now or never. "Your so-called Arsehole has kidnapped a young girl. *She* is the package." Rafferty heard the intake of breath on the other end of the line.

"Shit! That is serious."

"Very."

Withers grabbed the receiver. "Lucas, this is Sheriff Withers. Can we meet?"

"I don't think so!"

"Listen, I know that you killed Ralph Baxter."

There was silence on the other end.

"It had to be you, Lucas. You know as well as we do that the General has a specific target area for his killings..."

"Between the eyes," said Ty sadly, again thinking of his friend Leroy. "And chopping him up," he added bitterly.

Withers felt his pain. "I'm sorry, Lucas, but I need to save the life of *my* friend; and you can help."

Ty considered hanging up, but the life of a girl was too much of a draw. "What do you suggest?"

Withers looked at Rafferty, not for support but as a confirmation that this was *his* case. "A temporary amnesty."

Rafferty's face was a picture of dismay.

"Keep talking." Ty sounded unimpressed.

"We meet in open space, you and me. We talk. Then you walk."

"Just like that," responded Ty with heavy sarcasm.

"Just like that," confirmed Withers, his voice neutral, making it clear that this was going to be a business proposition rather than an emotional one. He waited for a reply.

"You think I can help you save this girl?"

"I don't know, Lucas, but I think you can help us get the General."

"No chance! He's mine."

Withers looked away, mumbling to himself. He had to get through somehow. Finally, he said, "Okay, agreed. You get the General – but first, you have to help us find the girl."

Rafferty exploded. "Are you fucking stupid or something? You can't give him the General. They're both wanted for murder…!"

Ty chuckled down the line. "You've upset the agent, sheriff. He won't let you stick to any deal."

Withers tightened his grip on the receiver and controlled his temper. "Trust me, Lucas, this is my ship. I have both hands on the rudder, and she goes where I want her to go. If it's straight up Agent Rafferty's arse, then so be it."

Rafferty could say nothing, but his expression said plenty.

"I like your style, sheriff. In another life…"

"Yeah, I hear you, Lucas. But I need an answer. My friend could be closer to death than we ever imagined."

Ty sensed the despair in his voice and softened. "An amnesty, you say?"

"Temporary," Withers emphasised.

Ty made him wait. "Okay. Where and when?"

****

It had taken a ridiculous amount of time to arrange, but now at last Judith was sitting opposite the man who had succeeded Leroy Figgis. She couldn't believe the hoops she had to jump through for this privilege, and she resented Raymond Ross for it. Her feelings weren't improved by the look of the man. True, he appeared a lot younger than he obviously was, and he had an aura about him which announced that here was a wealthy, successful member of the human race. It was just that he didn't come over as human. She thought of all the science fiction films she had ever watched, the ones with automatons and robots who looked real but weren't. *I, Raymond Ross*, she thought, sounds better than *I, Robot*.

He had not stood when she entered, as Leroy always did. He had not shaken her hand, offered pleasantries, or even a coffee. She could see that he wanted this over, and she was beginning to feel the same.

"Thank you for seeing me, Mr Ross."

His smile was enough to lower the temperature by several degrees. "You will appreciate that I cannot spare you too much time, Miss Wiseman."

"Oh, yes. You must be very busy following the death of…"

"Exactly." The silence was heavy. "Shall we begin?"

Judith took out her recorder and laid it on the desk.

"There will be no recording," he said sharply. "You may, of course, take notes."

"Thank you," she replied, shocked.

"But my lawyers will need to see all articles before publication."

"I don't think that will be necessary, Mr Ross. I just want to do a profile on you."

"Nevertheless, this is non-negotiable. Do you wish to continue?"

He found her rather attractive, in a blousy sort of way. Not at all like his Paulette, who wouldn't dream of wearing skirts quite that short, or heels quite that high. But he knew he had to be careful what he said. He had naturally carried out exhaustive checks on her, and they revealed a feisty woman who was good at her job and rarely took any kind of lip from her male counterparts. He had also learnt that she had been seen with the local sheriff, so any word out of place on his part could spell real disaster. Life was getting precarious indeed.

Judith made a point of returning the recorder to her handbag and took out her notepad and pencil. "You are in charge," she said, with a smile that hid her true feelings. "So, tell me about your relationship with Mr Figgis."

He waited a few moments before replying, his eyes small beneath a furrowed brow. "Off limits, I'm afraid."

"Sorry?"

"You are here to do a profile on me. That is what you said."

"I did, but…"

His eyes narrowed even more. "I will not discuss Mr Figgis."

Judith was surprised at this turn of events. "Why would that be, Mr Ross? He was your chairman…"

"He was. And now he has gone. Please continue."

She was getting angry now, the little flush to her cheeks announcing the imminent arrival of a runaway train, out of control and determined to flatten the smug man sitting at the desk in front of her. "Perhaps, then, you would care to comment on Mr Figgis's other occupation."

This time it was his turn to look surprised. "I don't know what you mean."

"I mean drug-dealing!" There, she had said it, and now she was going to reap the whirlwind.

"I beg your pardon!"

"I think you heard me, Mr Ross. I would like your take on the subject."

The colour had drained from his face, his eyes appearing sunken and dark. How on earth did she know about the drugs? Ross himself had only found out a week before Figgis went to the island, when the chairman had let something slip in an unguarded moment while talking about his brother Frank. Now, it was as if the whole world had been working on a massive jigsaw and the final pieces were about to be put in place, revealing Ross as the bad guy. "I have no idea..." he began, but she knew otherwise.

There is a whole new story here, she decided. "Were you part of this?"

Ross was catatonic with rage. His mouth opened, but nothing came out. Suddenly, he was on his feet. "Get out!" he finally screamed. "I want you out of here!"

Judith felt the force of his anger and stood, taking a step backwards. "I will continue my investigation, Mr Ross. You can be sure of that."

Ross shouted for his secretary, who raced into the room, dreading what she might find.

"Get her out – now!" he demanded, but Judith was already moving to the door. The secretary stood motionless, unsure of how to proceed. She had never seen Mr Ross like this before, and it frightened her. Judith's movement brought her to her senses, and she quickly guided the other woman through the door, for both their safety. She slammed the door and leant against it, catching her breath. "What have you done?" she gasped.

Judith had regained her composure. "Believe me, it will get a lot worse by the time I've finished with him." She turned, brushed down her skirt, and walked down the corridor, head held high.

Chapter Twenty-Nine

Chad Orwell had one more piece of information for the sheriff, and he decided he would deliver this one in person. He strolled into the police station and stopped at the desk. Deputy Janowski was on duty.

"Hello, Doug," Chad said. "Is the sheriff in?"

"Yes, sir. I'll let him know you're here."

"Never mind that, Doug. I'll introduce myself." He grinned and tapped the side of his nose. Dawg shrugged and let him go ahead. It was obviously some kind of a game these two men were playing.

Withers turned as his door opened, fully expecting Dawg to appear. When he saw it was Chad, he rose to shake his hand. Their grip was strong and close, as befitted men with a mutual respect for each other. Chad took a look around, as he always did.

"Just thought I'd slum it this time," he said with a straight face, as he always did.

Withers' grin was hollow. "Nice of you to come down to our level."

"It's okay, John. I'll have a shower when I get back home!"

Rafferty watched this pantomime with something akin to bewilderment, before both men broke into laughter and Chad handed over a folder.

"Report on your tyre mark and paint sliver from the Copper Ridge place," he said by way of explanation. "You might not be too surprised at the findings, after what you told me about your theories."

Withers opened the folder and began to read. "The paint matches the colour used by Toyota for their Camry range. The tyre mark matches tyres that are regulation fit on all Toyota vehicles." He read on, a grin creasing his face. "Good work, Chad. Thank you for this."

****

He found a parking space without too much trouble, to his great surprise, and entered the Mercurial Bank for the third time. It was tedious, but any pressure he could exert would be well worthwhile.

Judith was across the street in a small café, calming herself after her run-in with Ross and indulging in a cream cake and coffee. Her nerves needed calories to regroup. She looked through the window and waved at Withers, but he didn't see her.

She thought of chasing after him to tell her what she had done. Then she had an attack of common sense, and just watched him go into the bank. The last thing she wanted to do was antagonise the sheriff. No doubt, if she was wrong about Ross, word would soon get back to John Withers. She shivered at that prospect, no matter how unlikely it seemed to her. Ross was into something up to his vulpine eyes, she knew.

The receptionist watched Withers go direct to the lift and thought better of saying anything. She recognised the sheriff from his previous visits, and he didn't look too friendly today. She watched the lift door close and felt sorry for whoever was going to be on the receiving end.

The lift stopped at the top floor, and Withers said "Bollocks!" to the voice proclaiming his arrival. He stepped out and headed for the office, almost breaking down the door.

Ross was at his desk, jacket off, his tie loose and a glass of something in his hand. He looked flushed. No, more than that, he looked frenzied, as if something catastrophic had befallen him and he hadn't yet recovered. "What the fuck do you want now?" he demanded, his voice cracking with strain.

Despite being startled at the state of the man, Withers came straight to the point. "You have a fleet of Toyota Camrys."

Ross was confused at this opening gambit. "We have four Camrys, yes," he offered. "They are for the use of some of our employees."

"Where are they?"

"What?"

"Simple question, even for a banker," Withers sneered. "Where are they?"

"Well," Ross started, flustered, "I'm not sure."

Withers lent across the desk, his face well and truly in the vice-chairman's. "Let me help you, then. We know that one of them was used for an illegal entry to the Copper Ridge West estate. More specifically, leading to the property owned by your bank and leased to Ralph Baxter. Remember now?"

"I have no control over who uses our vehicles, sheriff." He stared back. "And I don't like your attitude, either."

Withers was sorely tempted to lift him out of his chair and toss him through the window, but that wouldn't register too highly on the scales of justice. "I don't like *you*, Mister Ross," he whispered through clenched teeth. "Let's call this strike three… and you're out."

Withers stormed out of the room, almost taking the door with him as he burst through, causing the secretary to scream and Ross to sink even lower into his plush office chair.

He knew his days were numbered.

****

Withers loved this lake so much. He fished in it, swam in it, barbecued on its shore and thought of Heather every time the sun set while he was sitting on a tree trunk, drinking a cool beer. She had been so much to him: wife, carer, friend. After her loss, there was only a huge hole, an abyss so wide that no bridge would ever straddle it. Or so he thought. But suddenly there seemed to be a beacon throwing light into the depths, filling him with renewed hope. His thoughts now were of Judith Wiseman.

He still couldn't explain the hold she had over him. He was a grown man, for heaven's sake! Not some whimsical teenager, gingerly dipping his toe into the love pool. He watched a gull circling and smiled. That was just what he had been doing – going around in circles without any planned final destination. Now, at long last, was his chance to land and settle.

"Sheriff Withers."

Without turning, Withers said, "Lucas Black." He stood and waited for the other man to show himself.

Stepping out from behind a tree, Ty said, "I go by the name of Ty now."

"Okay… Ty. Do you want to sit?"

266

They sat beside each other on the rough-hewn timber bench, its surface inscribed with initials and hearts from long-ago trysts.

"Very fitting, sheriff. A love seat," said Ty with a smile.

"Don't get too comfortable. This isn't a declaration of undying affection."

"To business then," said Ty. "What are you offering?"

"Like I said: you help me save the girl, and you get the Arsehole. Simple."

"If only it were," sighed Ty.

Withers took a breath. "Look, I've studied your history. I've read up so much that I know more about you than you do yourself. You're basically a good man."

Ty couldn't help a grunt of derision. "Shucks, sheriff," he said in a mock-teen voice, "you sure know how to sweet-talk a girl."

"Let's talk about Figgis," said Withers.

"What about him?"

"I don't understand… how could a man like that get away with drug-running without anyone getting a whiff of it?"

Lucas laughed. "You think he was a baron or something? Hell, man, you sure didn't know Leroy."

"So tell me."

Lucas sat back on the bench, a faraway look in his eyes, remembering. "I'd worked with Leroy before, and he had only ever dealt in minor things…"

"Like diamonds."

"Yeah, he'd picked up a few sparklers once, paying under the odds and saving on a bit of tax, but that was all."

"So why the drugs?"

"That's what I never did understand. None of us knew anything about it until the handover. I swear that was the one and only time." After a pause, Ty added, "He did say that he had done it for Frank, but that made no sense either."

"Frank was his brother – half-brother, actually – died of a drug overdose."

"Ah," said Ty, finally understanding. "That's why he wanted to burn it all."

"What?" Withers was astounded.

"He just wanted to destroy it, sheriff. For Frank."

Withers could say nothing. His view of Leroy Figgis had been based on one thing only: drugs. And now he knew the truth, he suddenly felt sickened to his stomach. "Tell me exactly what happened on the island."

It took Ty some time to gather his thoughts and relay them to the sheriff. It all became so vivid as he recalled each event as if it had happened just yesterday: the despair in Leroy's eyes as the General drove away with the drugs and the hate in his own heart as he pumped two bullets into the body he thought was the General. When he had finished, he sat back, exhausted.

Withers waited a moment as it all sank in. "So, the General *had* been wounded. That was what the first payment was for."

"What payment?" said Ty.

"It's okay," said Withers, "I'm just thinking out loud." He cleared his head. "Does the name Ray or Raymond Ross mean anything?"

Ty thought about it. "The Arsehole may have mentioned a Ray at one point, but it didn't mean much to me."

"Think about it. Was Figgis present when he said the name Ray?"

"No, that I *can* remember. We were in the bunks, and he was going on about prison. None of us had a clue what he was talking about. But Leroy wasn't there, that I know."

Withers felt the smallest flutter of triumph. "So, Figgis never knew that it was Ross who was out to get him."

Ty looked at the lawman. "Sorry?"

"It's nothing." Withers considered for a moment, before adding, "You ought to know that the General did ten years for killing his father."

Ty gave a grim smile. "A bullet through the temple, I assume."

Withers nodded, and they sat there in silence, each deep within their own thoughts.

Eventually, Ty got up and offered his hand to Withers, who took it. "I think you've helped more than you know," Withers said. "Thanks." Then he had another thought. "This meeting tomorrow…"

"What about it?"

"You're not going to tell me where it is, I know, but can you offer me a crumb here? Where did Piers and Cameron used to meet up?"

Ty walked away, smiling. "You want a crumb, sheriff? Okay, here it is. The 'P' isn't Piers. So long. I'll see what I can drag out of the Arsehole before I put him where he belongs."

"I'm not going to let you do that, Ty," said Withers, but the other man had already disappeared through the trees.

****

It was late, but Withers had a lot to chew over. He sat at his desk, sucking on an extra strong, his mind in turmoil. The murky waters were starting to clear, and he was piecing it all together. Yes, the General was after Lucas Black, but the murder of Leroy Figgis had been planned from the moment the General set foot back in the country. Raymond Ross had paid for his operation, and then paid him again for the slaying of Figgis. It was a clever twist, making the killings appear part of the revenge scenario; but, like Lucas had said, Leroy Figgis was an innocent in all of this. The General had no need or desire to kill Figgis or the others. It was Lucas Black he was after. That's all.

Withers' mind turned to Millie Moody, and another thought suddenly struck him. Reaching for the phone, he wondered where Rafferty was, but it was only a cursory thought. He had more important things to occupy him.

The phone connected and a voice answered, "Special Agent Murphy."

"It's Sheriff John Withers here."

"Yes, sir."

"Can you do something for me, Agent Murphy?"

"Andy, sir."

"Andy, yes. I need you to check through the property portfolio of the Mercurial Bank..."

"Yes, sir."

"Especially isolated farm buildings and unoccupied steads around Bakerton and its surrounds."

****

Rafferty came into the office and pulled up the spare chair. Withers had never seen such a thing and whistled through his teeth. "Well, it must have been some day, Pat. You – sitting down!"

"Tell me about it."

"So, where have you been? I've missed you."

"That's a mighty big lake, John."

Withers sat up. "You've been at the lake?"

"I sure as hell have! I wasn't going to let you get away with talking to Lucas Black without close attendance."

"That's very thoughtful of you. I'm touched," said Withers with a smile.

"You most certainly are!" retorted Rafferty. "Did you really think I'd let you talk to Black without me being there?"

"Don't tell me you tried to follow him," Withers said. "I made a promise."

"Yeah, you did," spat Rafferty with some venom, "but I sure as hell didn't. Godsake, John, he's a felon!"

"So, where'd he go?"

Rafferty became sullen. "We lost him."

Withers guffawed with delight. "You have the finest men and women in the country – and you still lost him!"

Before either man could continue, the phone rang, and Withers lifted the receiver, a grin still etched on his face.

"Sheriff? It's Andy Murphy. I've raised a list for you. There are six properties in total, some of which have been empty for over fifty years. It seems the bank isn't too desperate to sell them on."

"Can you get the details over to me?"

"Already emailed, sir."

"Thanks, Andy, great job."

Rafferty watched intently as Withers put down the phone. "Something important?" he asked.

"I think so," replied Withers. "Listen, Pat, if you were the General, and you had a girl hostage, where would you keep her?"

Rafferty pondered a moment before replying. "Somewhere quiet and unobtrusive."

"Right. And if you had the backing of a top banker who could offer you just such a place, you'd be stupid not to use it."

"You certainly would," agreed Rafferty. "I take it Andy Murphy supplied you with a list of bank properties."

"Yes, he did. But it's no good us going off half-cocked. If we checked all these places out tonight, the General or his thugs would see us coming a mile away, and probably kill Millie long before we got there. Can you arrange simultaneous raids for first thing in the morning, Pat?"

Rafferty nodded. "Leave it to me."

"And I'll need an arrest warrant for one Raymond Ross, deputy chairman of the Mercurial Bank."

"Is that it?" queried Rafferty, watching the sheriff with something akin to admiration.

"No, there's something else… something Lucas Black told me. It wasn't Piers who met up with 'C', as we thought."

"So, who was it?" asked Rafferty.

"I have a good idea. One phone call is all I need…"

Chapter Thirty

They met at his place for the first time. They sat in the garden, him with a beer and her with an iced lemonade, with a fresh strawberry floating in it. Decadence personified, she thought dreamily. A nice touch. She lifted out the strawberry and took a bite, the fruit juice trickling down the sides of her mouth. Withers leant forward and dabbed her lips with a napkin, then reached further over and kissed her tenderly. She responded, caressing his face with both hands as if she wanted to make sure he didn't move away. There was no chance of that.

Finally, they came up for air, and both sat back in their chairs, their eyes locked.

"I didn't think something like this would ever happen to me again," he said, his voice faltering.

Judith smiled. "I know the feeling," she said, picking up her glass and offering a toast. He tapped it with his beer bottle. "To us."

"To us," he echoed, "wherever it takes us."

"Amen to that," she said, savouring her drink.

They sat in silence then, just like an old married couple, snug in their togetherness, and not needing words to communicate.

Finally, he said, "I think we are nearly there."

"Are we?" asked Judith, bemused.

"The Figgis case," he explained.

"Oh, that," she said without feeling. "Why, what's happened?"

He stirred in his seat, his enthusiasm boundless. "We have a few locations where Millie might be…"

"That's good," she said.

"And we are close to finding the General."

"Wonderful! So, it will soon be all over," she offered, hoping to heaven that was the case. She needed time with Withers, to bring Heather out and to join her as someone whom he could love. She would never replace Heather, she knew, but she just wanted the opportunity to *share* him. She put down her glass. "John, can I ask you something?"

"Anything."

She paused, choosing her words. "I… I would very much like to stay with you tonight."

His face was crestfallen. "I would like that, too. But it's impossible…"

"Because of Heather?" she asked, knowing the answer he would give. But she was wrong.

"No. Not because of Heather. Believe me. I want you to, more than anything, but tomorrow…"

"It's okay, John, I understand. Work comes first."

They were silent once more, until Judith said, "I really do understand, John. Life with a policeman is never going to be a bed of roses. I can wait. Besides, I have my own job to think about."

He squeezed her hand, both with affection and relief. "So, what exclusive are you working on now?"

"It's an exposé!" she exclaimed, her excitement showing.

Withers was happy for her, and leaned over, planting a kiss on her cheek. "Really! And who, may I ask, are you exposing?"

"Raymond Ross!"

Withers sat back, his shoulders sagging. "What?"

"The man's a monster, John. I went to see him today, and..."

"You saw him?"

"Just before you did, actually," she said. "I saw you going into the bank."

"I didn't know..."

"I was having a coffee. I needed something after meeting him. He's a... a cretin!" Her beautiful face scrunched up and her eyes grew bigger than he'd ever seen them. "I've already got so much background info... I'm going to feed him to the dogs, John."

Withers knew he was going to upset her, but there was nothing he could do about that. He grabbed her hand and held it tight. "You can't do that, Judith," he said. "Ross is ours."

She stared at him with incredulity, but could think of nothing to say.

DAY SEVEN

Chapter Thirty-One

Raymond Ross had suffered a sleepless night. He had looked over at his darling Paulette, love of his life and wife for the last blissful seventeen years. He stirred in bed and sat up, feeling no sleep in his eyes, only confusion in his soul.

It had all seemed so easy. He had hated the angelic Leroy Figgis with a passion, seeing in him all the good things that Ross himself craved but didn't possess. Leroy was popular, ebullient, charismatic. He ran the bank with such precision that the other board members needed to do nothing; just sit back and bask in the reflected glory. But that wasn't enough for Ross. He needed power. He needed Paulette to respect him, as well as worship the very ground he walked on. No, Leroy Figgis really did have to go.

He put on his dressing gown and tiptoed down the hall, carefully opening the second bedroom door and peeking in. He saw his son Carl, twelve years old and school athletics champion, a spitting image of his late uncle, sleeping soundly, his iPhone clutched in his hand, as always. Ross went into the room and carefully took the phone, placing it on the bedside cabinet. He had thought of leaving a last message on it but decided that would be too cruel.

He wasn't sure when the idea to do away with Figgis had first come to him – probably when the Spaniard had phoned to say that Billy was in trouble and needed urgent funds. Ross hadn't heard from Billy for some time and hadn't been convinced the call was genuine, so he had made Billy come to the phone, even though he was so obviously in agony. With confirmation of the authenticity of the request, the money had been transferred immediately, so Billy could undergo an urgent operation in whatever far-flung place he had ended up. Ross didn't want to know all the details; he just wanted to know when Billy would be well enough to repay the debt. By killing Leroy. It had taken a surprisingly long time and an inordinate amount of money. Ross had wondered whether Billy had been stringing him along; but eventually he had turned up at Ross's door, looking for more money and a place to stay. He had given Billy the keys to Murton's Farm, an empty smallholding out of town and off the radar of the bank accountants.

The plan became operational when Ross found out that there was to be a meeting at the Colonial House, so all he had to do was persuade the housekeeper to let the General in. A few notes would settle that. It didn't matter to Ross how many of them died, as long as one of them was left alive to tell the world that the murders had been committed out of revenge, and he, Raymond Ross, would be in the clear and would be crowned the new chairman of the Mercurial Bank.

It had been only after the killings that the General had informed him that Murton's Farm wasn't good enough accommodation any more and had insisted on an upgrade. Ross had been assured that Baxter had been spared and, after seeing the cops, he would quietly disappear. The Copper Ridge West property was therefore suddenly vacant. What harm would it do, letting the General stay there for a few days?

But no, it soon became apparent that Billy couldn't even do the job right! He'd massacred the lot of them and even cut up Leroy. That hadn't been part of the deal, and Ross felt that the General was playing games with him. He had to die for such treachery.

Returning to his bedroom, Ross quickly slipped into his hunting clothes, taking one last loving look at Paulette.

He moved quietly downstairs and into the study, his steps both silent and heavy. He considered writing a note but had no idea what to say, so he went to the gun cabinet, unlocked it and took out his favourite hunting rifle, along with a box of high-velocity shells. He was after more than stags this time.

****

The two Shangri-las bore no resemblance to each other. The one in Lanscarges – the brothel – was all glitz and bling, albeit on a very tawdry and cheap level. It had dazzling glitterballs in the reception area, where scantily-clad young girls stroked the legs of potential clients and pouted exotically while ordering watered-down champagne by the bucket-load at extortionate prices for the men and sipping sparkling water themselves. The air was still thick with cigarette and cigar smoke, despite the supposed worldwide ban on such substances inside buildings. Nobody cared. They just wanted to have fun, the men getting legs over and the girls pocketing their ten percent of the fee charged by management. These were well-paid girls by any standards.

The other Shangri-La was a poky little club in a poky little back street in poky downtown Bakerton. Ty Cobden stood across the street, surveying the grim exterior of the run-down building, its brickwork in urgent need of repair and the wooden window frames desperate for a lick of paint. The

Shangri-La sign, once neon-lit, hung sadly on one and a half brackets, its lettering stained and pretty near unreadable to the untrained eye. The adjoining houses looked in similar disrepair, their windows boarded up and peeling paint on the doors. Hiram Baker would be turning in his grave at the desecration of this area of his beautiful town.

A couple of teen girls hovered by the club door, puffing heavily on cigarettes and giggling, forever hoisting up their microskirts to reveal as much of their knickers as they dared, until a group of five boys arrived and whisked them inside. To Ty, it seemed like he was about to enter a crèche.

He had been standing there for almost an hour, and it was now ten to midday. He hadn't seen the General or anybody who might conceivably be associated with him. The club was offering a lunch-time happy hour, with buy-one-get-one-free offers on everything but the hardest liquor, so it was fairly busy, with mainly youngsters going through the door, even though Ty suspected many of them should have been at school. The pistol tucked into his sock rubbed against his trouser leg, and he felt secure, despite the Arsehole's warning to come unarmed. Even he must have known that Ty wouldn't be *that* stupid.

Making his way into the club, Ty couldn't believe the noise. The reception foyer wasn't so bad – but when the door to the club proper opened, a cacophony of noise belched forth, assaulting ears and every other sensory organ in the human body. He could even feel his teeth rattling.

At least when the door was shut, Ty could hear the girl at the small counter. "Membership card," she said, gum oozing out of the corner of her mouth.

"I'm new," said Ty, smiling sweetly.

"Cute," said the girl, "but you ain't comin' in without a card."

"So sell me one."

"Gotta be nominated by a member," she explained, then blew a nicely rounded bubble.

Ty looked around and saw a thin, pasty-faced girl leaning against the wall. He went up to her and took out a couple of notes from his wallet. "Hi," he said, as she turned to look at him.

She gave him a wide smile, whether as a greeting to him or because she'd seen the money, he couldn't be sure, but he had a good idea. "Hi," she replied, leaning back ever so slightly so that her pert breasts lifted a little. She'd been seeing too many reality shows.

"I wonder if you would do me a favour?" said Ty.

"I'm not that sort of girl."

"I can see that," he said quickly, "but I'm just after a nomination."

"Is that what they call it these days?" She giggled at the innuendo.

Ty shrugged. "I'd like to become a member, and I hoped you would put me forward." He waved the money in front of her.

"Sure," she said, grabbing the notes and sashaying up to the counter, her thin legs making her look like a heron in a purple skirt and pink stockings. "Hey," she announced, "he's with me."

"Okay. There's the tariffs."

Ty liked that. A touch of class in an otherwise crap place. She could have said 'price list', but she went all up-market. "I'll take the 'casual membership'," he told her, handing over the required fee. She waved him away with another gum bubble, this one bursting across her mouth with a lilac splurge. Ty ignored it and opened the door to the club proper.

The soundproofing must have been top-notch because the wall of sound only hit him as he stepped over the threshold. He blinked at the strobe lighting, seeing figures dancing before him like in a silent movie, their faces highlighted by a myriad of colours created by plastic and computer wizardry. They looked for all the world like a Technicolor zombie ensemble, gyrating to the music of The Futureheads. Not Ty's choice, but he couldn't help rocking to the beat as he jostled past the crowd to a position where he could take a look around. He couldn't believe that it was the middle of the day and yet these kids were already letting it all hang out. Man, he was past it!

He got a few blank stares from the regular members, but he just put that down to jealousy. He found a pillar in the centre of the dancefloor and leant against it as nonchalantly as he could. Cool dude, on the lookout…

Sitting on a bar stool, sipping a green liquid through a straw, Number Two had seen Ty enter, his eyes following him warily. He knew what this Lucas was capable of, so he intended to take no chances. He waited a full five minutes before he rose and made his way to the pillar, pushing aside the young people who got in his way. The sooner he was out of this place, the better.

Ty had sensed the other man's approach, although he didn't at first recognise him. The thing that really gave the game away was that these two were way older than anybody else in the club, so Ty knew what was coming.

"Glad you could make it, Lucas."

Ty swivelled, meeting Number Two face to face for the first time in four years. But still it didn't register.

"You look puzzled, *mi amigo*. Although I confess that I have changed over the years. No beard and long hair, as you can see."

"Number Two," said Ty, finally realising. "I think I preferred you when your face was covered!"

"You always were the *cómico*, Lucas. Shall we take a walk?"

Ty took a long drink and looked hard at the other man. "Where's the girl?"

"Come," growled Number Two, pushing Ty roughly towards the door. "Outside we will talk."

The girl on reception gave Ty a strange look as the two men emerged, Number Two gripping his arm tightly. "You didn't stay long," she said, eyelashes flashing at speed as if she was sending out a Morse code message.

Ty winked. "Wasn't in the mood for dancing, sweetheart. See you later."

When they emerged into the midday sun, Ty blinked. The artificial light had caused black spots to dance before his eyes, and the music seemed to have seared the very core of his eardrums. Number Two looked even more uncomfortable.

"Man," Number Two groaned, "I've just spent three hours in there, waiting for you. It's a *pesadillo!*" When Ty looked bewildered, he translated, "A nightmare, *mi amigo.*"

Ty nodded. "I don't know how they cope, these youngsters."

"You are getting old, like all of us," said Number Two with a grin; and, despite the circumstances, Ty thought he might even start liking this guy.

"So, what's your name? Number Two is far too formal for someone who is aiming to kill me."

Number Two was clearly shocked. "Oh, no, *señor*, you have that all wrong. It is not I who wants you dead, only the *General*." His deep Spanish accent wove itself around the last word, making it sound far more sinister than it actually was, although that was bad enough. "My name is Hector," he added, his accent omitting the initial letter.

"*Ector*," repeated Ty with a pale imitation of the Spanish inflection, "I am Ty."

"Ah, no longer Lucas, then."

"That was a world ago. Until the Arsehole came back."

Hector laughed loudly. "Arsehole! *Dios mío*, that is a wonderful name for him!" He stopped mid-guffaw. "But you must treat him with respect, also."

"That's probably the wrong word, Ector. But I know what you mean."

They walked slowly along Pickett Street, before turning left down Penn Avenue, Hector guiding Ty with his arm against his back. Despite the good humour, Ty knew very well that the Spaniard had a gun pressed against him. It was incongruous that the laughter continued. "I am sure, my friend, that you are armed," said Hector between chuckles.

Ty was surprised by the question. He expected to be frisked at some time, so there wouldn't be any sense in denying it. "Of course."

"Good. I would like it to be a *lucha justa*... you know, a fair fight. Much as I love the *General* dearly, I was not happy with the way he despatched *señor* Figgis and his friends. I would not wish the same for you."

"Thanks for that."

"Oh, do not get me wrong, my friend," said Hector, suddenly very serious. "I expect you to be killed, but at least I would have no, how do you say, *qualms* about it."

They walked on in silence until Hector indicated a green saloon parked by the kerb. "Please get in, Ty. We have a little journey to make."

****

As Hector's car pulled out into the traffic, he didn't notice a Volvo estate slip in a couple of cars behind. The driver was Deputy Phil Lenier, and Dawg Janowski was riding shotgun. In the back, eyes half-closed, was John Withers. They were all dressed as civilians, but each packed their standard weapons in holsters beneath their jackets.

"Phil, I hope this old heap of scrap will keep up," Withers said sarcastically.

Lenier snorted. "Don't worry, boss, I won't lose them."

"Good," said Withers, and fell silent. After Lucas's tip-off, it hadn't taken much to work out who 'P' and 'C' were, and a phone call to the safe house confirmed everything. Christina had told him the name of Pandando's club, and Withers naturally knew all about the Bakerton equivalent.

Now it was just a waiting game.

****

The General was growing impatient. It had taken four long years, and now it was all coming to fruition. Suddenly, those long months of agony and recovery were being despatched to the back of his mind with the knowledge that the man who was responsible would soon be squirming at his feet, begging forgiveness and mercy. He would hear the pleas with a sweet taste of pleasure, before placing a cross on the creep's forehead and embedding a bullet in the centre, wiping away long-held memories of his father and the wrongs that had been done to him over the years. Yes, here was the final cleansing of Billy Rhodes...

****

"So," said Ty, "what have you been doing these last four years?"

Hector smiled. "You are making the small talk, I think. In truth, I have been looking after the sick and infirm, *mi amigo*."

"You mean the General."

"*Si*, he was in a bad way. You put a bullet very close to his spine."

"That wasn't me, Ector. That was Ralphie."

"The youngster? A good shot, no?"

"I'd say lucky rather than good. But then again, it wasn't good enough, was it?"

Hector understood Ty's meaning and belly-laughed, his hands slipping dangerously from the wheel. "You mean, he should have killed the *General*! Yes, yes, I can see how that was not so lucky for you." He regained control of the car and took a left turn in one movement, the wheels screeching as one of the tyres mounted the pavement, causing an elderly couple to do an arthritic shuffle out of the way.

"Learn to drive in Barcelona, did you?" asked Ty, tongue firmly in cheek.

Hector looked at him. "You make fun of my driving?"

"Well, if you want the General to kill me, perhaps you should slow down a little."

Hector was still looking at him, the road forgotten. It took agonising seconds before he realised where he was, and he took evasive action as a car pulled out of a side road. He thought nothing of it and continued on his merry way.

"So," said Ty, catching his breath, "how did the General get fixed up? It must have taken serious money."

"Oh, yes, that it did. The *General* has a wealthy benefactor, I think you call it. He paid for everything... including my long stay in a very nice hotel, thank you very much." Hector waved both arms to indicate the shape of a beautiful woman. "Including all the modern cons, as you say," he added without necessity. Ty understood fully.

"It must have taken a long time," said Ty, trying to piece together how the Arsehole had got to this moment.

"Oh, yes. He was convalesced for many, many months. It was go and touch for a while." Hector was grinning all the while, happy to have somebody else to talk to. This guy Ty was okay by him. Pity it's not going to last too long, he thought almost sadly.

"So, where's the girl?"

Hector almost braked with the shock of the question. "I cannot tell you that! The *General* would not be a happy bunny – is that what you call it?"

"Is he going to let her go, Ector?"

"I cannot say, *mi amigo*. Who knows how his brainbox works?"

"You have to tell me where she is, so we can save her. It's not necessary for the Arsehole to kill her. He'll have me."

Hector nodded. "Yes, I know that. But he is my *jefe*, my boss." The car abruptly turned left into a dirt track and came to a halt, skidding slightly on the mud. "We are here. You can talk to the *General* yourself now," Hector said, throwing open the door and jumping out. It was only then that Ty noticed that he hadn't been wearing his seatbelt. Madman!

"Come," Hector ordered, now waving his pistol in the air. "We walk the rest of the way."

Ty looked at his surroundings. Fields, and more fields, stretching out as far as the eye could see, their colours a swathe of greens, pale yellows and the deepest browns. Marking the extent of the dirt track on one side was a laurel hedge, presumably planted by a long-forgotten farmer. On the other side was a fence comprised of coppiced wood, skilfully woven and as sturdy as the hedge opposite, and probably built by an artisan for the same farmer. Ty marvelled at the ingenuity of man… and the horrors perpetrated in the name of man. He thought of Ralphie Baxter and wished that he could go back and undo everything. *Especially* Ralphie…

"You must walk faster, Ty," demanded Hector, waving the pistol even more, his finger round the trigger.

****

Lenier stopped the car just before the turning. The three of them got out and looked up the dirt track, keeping back as much as possible. Dawg pushed away some branches and read a weathered sign. "Colebrook Farm," he said.

"One of the bank's properties. Millie Moody may be here, too," said Withers, more with hope than confidence. Millie could equally be... He tried not to think the worst.

They saw the two men ahead, Ty and whoever, walking briskly, the pistol clearly visible as it was waved in the air.

"Take it slow, lads," ordered Withers, unclipping his revolver. The deputies did likewise. "No heroics."

After a few moments, they began to follow the others, keeping a safe distance and a watchful eye on the man with the gun. He could be very dangerous.

****

The General could hear them coming, and his heart began to race. At the same time, the deep wound in his back began to tingle, and he knew this would be his reward for the agony he had endured. He was grateful for the help offered by Ray, but the price demanded for his medical treatment had been unexpected. He often wondered whether Ray might try to kill him to tie up all the loose ends, but that wouldn't work, because some pretty incriminating evidence had been lodged with a personal friend of the General's. Once Lucas Black had been eliminated, Billy Rhodes could milk the new chairman of Mercurial Bank for as long as he liked. Life doesn't get any better than that.

****

Ty could see in the distance that the track was beginning to fan out into some kind of a courtyard, and there was what looked to be a ramshackle building beyond that. It was at that second that he appeared to twist his ankle. He went down, striking the ground harder than he had intended, but it gave him the chance he needed to slip out his revolver from his sock.

Hector looked concerned. "Are you okay, *mi amigo*? What has happened?"

Ty came back up with such speed that Hector could do nothing as a gun was held to his throat.

"This has happened, my friend," said Ty through tight lips. "Drop your gun and continue walking. If the General notices anything, you'll be the first to die."

Hector did not like that idea and hastily threw his gun into the hedge. He would get even later.

They carried on walking...

****

Lenier retrieved the gun when the policemen reached the spot. They had seen everything, and Withers marvelled at the speed Ty had demonstrated. He knew his creaking bones wouldn't allow him to do something like that, so he was pretty impressed. Ty would have made one hell of a policeman.

"We must be getting close," said Withers. "Phil, get through that fence and come up on the right. Dawg, see if there's any way through that hedge. I want a three-pronged attack."

The deputies nodded and set off. Withers watched Ty and the other man approach what looked like an enclosure of some kind, perhaps the long-forgotten front garden to the farmhouse. He stopped, spellbound. There, stepping into view, was the man responsible for everything. At last, he could see Billy Rhodes – the General.

Chapter Thirty-Two

Alby was in a happy place. He had thought long and hard about what he was going to give Millie for lunch. He knew she liked an omelette, so he had been foraging for things to go into it: nettles, cleavers, common mallow. They were all boiling away in a billy, the lid bouncing almost excitedly as the steam made its way out. He'd add the wild mushrooms later. Alby put a few more twigs on the fire and then sat on his rickety folding chair, surveying his domain.

You know, he thought, it was a blessing meeting Billy the General. It had changed Alby's life in so many wondrous ways. For a start, he had a friend for life, even if Billy did boss him around a little too much. But he could live with that, if it meant he could spend days like this. Ingesting the sights and sounds of a countryside untouched by human hand for hundreds of years. Okay, that might not be strictly true – there had been a farmer here some years ago, because of the buildings – but the principle still held. It was the silence that mattered most to Alby. And the beautiful girl locked up in the old farmhouse, of course. He contemplated the thought of letting her eat al fresco for once. She'd like that.

His thoughts went back to the General. Billy had told him once why he'd chosen that name. What was it now? Something about an old movie he once saw. Yes, that was it! Billy had seen a really old black-and-white movie once, starring a steam train! He had said it was big and powerful, the way he had felt sometimes. Anyways, he said it was way better than being called Billy! Alby had to agree with that but could never come up with a name for himself. Perhaps he'd ask Millie over lunch; she would find a name for him.

The fire crackled and spat as the boiling water dribbled down on to it, almost masking the distant sound – but Alby heard it. He listened. There it was again: the distinct sound of someone moving through the next field. Billy, Alby thought; that will be Billy. He'll be hungry. I'll just get him some...

He rose, intent on more foraging, and then heard a crack and a whine, and sensed a sudden, unexpected feeling. He looked down... and saw a mass of blood, and two fingers hanging by threads from his hand. He couldn't believe what he was looking at and staggered back, with the shock and nausea filling his body. He gasped and turned away, starting to run to the farmhouse. No, this can't be happening. "Billy!" he screamed, as another bullet came his way.

****

Millie had been lying on the bed when she heard the first shot, and jumped up, fear etched on her face. This was it: she was going to die. For a fleeting second, she thought that Alby would protect her, but the sound of the second bullet threw that possibility into turmoil. What the hell was going on?

She rushed to the door and rattled the handle, knowing that it was locked, but praying that by some miracle it would fly open and she could make her escape.

She heard Alby outside, shouting, "Billy!"

Fuck Billy, she thought angrily, what about me? She banged on the door and screeched, her voice sounding distant and so very weak. "Alby!" she shouted. "Let me out! Let me out!"

Suddenly, she heard the key turn in the lock, and her defences went up. What if it isn't Alby? What if it's this Billy coming to finish her off? She stepped back from the door, frantically looking around for some kind of weapon. Stupid girl, she scolded herself, there's nothing here!

She was frozen in time, defenceless, helpless. The door swung open on rusty hinges, the sound reminding her of fingernails scraping down a blackboard. How could she think of something like that at a time like this? She was going insane. This was the end of her world.

"Millie," Alby called out, "it's me. I don't understand what's happening." The door was wide open, and he stood before her, holding up his left arm with the mangled hand, blood still dripping from the ends of his fingers. He was looking at it, sobbing loudly between each heavy breath, his face white and his wide eyes lost.

Millie, too, was in shock, but she knew they had to get away. She didn't have time for questions, so she ran out of the room, dragging Alby with her, stopping only momentarily at the front door to analyse what was facing them. She saw a figure climbing through a fence some way off and knew that they could reach the woods if they sprinted. She pulled Alby out with her, and they began the mad dash to safety, Alby blubbering and stumbling, his hand throbbing and his heart racing.

Raymond Ross saw them and stopped in his tracks. This wasn't right. Where the hell did that girl come from? He was after Billy Rhodes, not some slip of a girl. It didn't make sense. He'd only ever shot at stags before, and now here he was chasing down two people who didn't even register on his radar.

Obviously, the man was working for Billy, but the girl…?

Ross didn't have time to debate things. He'd already got himself in too far, and there was no way out. He steadied himself and raised the rifle to his shoulder. It was decision time: did he go for the girl or the wounded animal? He couldn't believe that he had already fired off two of his valuable bullets without bringing down his prey. The second shot hadn't even been close. He was losing his touch. He grimaced as his finger circled the trigger, held his breath, as all good marksmen do, and fired. You always despatch the wounded one first.

Millie and Alby heard the crack, and both instinctively looked round. Then he stopped in mid-stride and clutched his neck with his good hand, feeling warm liquid pump through his fingers. Millie screamed as Alby fell to his knees, the high-velocity bullet going right through his neck and embedding itself in a tree a few metres away. So near, was Alby's last thought in this world, and he slumped forward, mouthing the word 'Millie' as he did so.

Millie stood frozen to the spot, until she saw the man lower the gun and start to come after her. With one last desperate lunge, she crashed through the undergrowth and into the relative safety of the trees, knowing this was only the beginning of her ordeal. She so wished her pa was here beside her.

Racing past swinging branches, she went on, her lungs ready to burst, but knowing she had to keep going. Death was pursuing her, and she wasn't ready for that yet.

Stopping to catch her breath and listen, she heard a faint voice, calling her. "Millie! Millie Moody! This is Special Agent Jacob Abrahams." Pause. "If you can hear me, try to come towards my voice." Pause. "I'll keep talking. Millie!"

"I don't think so!" she whispered to herself between gritted teeth and ran in the opposite direction.

****

Raymond Ross also stopped. What the hell? How did a special agent get on his tail so quickly? Everything was out of control. He had come here to finish off the General once and for all, and here he was being pursued by officers of the law. He was in two minds as to what he should do: go after the girl or get rid of the agent. But what if there was more than one of them? Stupid, of course there will be others. But, so what? He had nothing to lose now, so he started off in the direction of the voice, stopping every few steps to gauge the position of this special agent.

Agent Abrahams was on his first field operation. He had passed top of class and had received ringing endorsements from the highest echelons of the agency. He was so proud. But foolhardy. One of the other agents close by warned him about showing himself, but he knew better. He could not understand why Millie had not responded, so he continued shouting, because he was there to save her, protect her from the evil she was facing. "Mil…"

The bullet sent him sprawling, the pain in his chest growing in intensity as he fell. He had felt nothing like it before. Training could never replicate the agony he was feeling now, and he so wanted it to end.

He heard more shots, but they sounded so distant, so beyond his sphere of consciousness. Then he was being manhandled, as gently as possible, by two pairs of hands, and he could hear a voice. "Man down. Murton's Farm. Ambulance!" And then he died.

Ross had made a swift withdrawal after firing the one bullet. He'd hit the man for sure, but a volley from some other agents had sent him scurrying for shelter. He stopped for a second, listening, then continued on the trail of the girl. She had headed for the woods, and he knew where that would eventually lead. There was no rush… he would get her in the end.

****

The wood was thick and threatening. Millie forced her way through the bracken and tree roots, too scared to stop. She heard the shots, but no more voices. Confused, she knew she had no option but to keep on going, wherever it led.

Stopping once more to catch her breath, she looked around. To most points of the compass, there were only trees; but to her left, she could see a trail leading past some huge oaks and out into a less-wooded glade, where the sun dappled through the branches and she could almost sense safety. With renewed vigour, she set off down the trail.

Breaking out of cover, Millie stopped, bent over with hands on knees, her breath escaping in hoarse gasps. After a few seconds, she straightened and studied her location. She was in a clearing all right, but it was full of timber logs, chopped down in their prime and left to rot. She was at one of the old abandoned sawmills up on Copper Ridge! Miles from home… and safety.

She listened for any discernible sound. Nothing. But she wasn't stupid. Whoever had killed Alby wasn't going to let her live, that was for sure. Then a thought struck her. What do they have at sawmills? Chainsaws and axes, that's what! Frantically, she scurried around, looking for some kind of defence. There were no buildings close by, so she had to hope that the workers had just dropped their tools and left. How likely was that, eh? She mentally kicked herself for her negative thoughts, and carried on looking.

****

He could see the sun through the trees and knew he was close. He'd been able to make quicker progress than the girl, so he was confident she would still be in the clearing somewhere. He shouldered the rifle and edged forward, eyes peeled. He didn't want to kill anybody else, but he had no alternative. He had decided long ago that Leroy had to go, and now so did the General. That would have been the end. But no, there were complications. There were always bloody complications. He could handle them in the bank, across his huge oak desk – but in real life? No, that was just impossible. He stifled a sob and carried on, ready to do the deed. After all, it was a straight choice: the girl's life or his security with Paulette. No competition.

He was in the open now, clearly visible to the girl if she was still there, but it didn't matter. She was scared, and he was armed.

****

Millie watched intently as he approached. He looked so… *normal*. Aside from the hunting gear he wore, he could have been one of her friendly neighbours. Like Mr Epstein. Yes, very much like Mr Epstein. Kindly and benevolent. Not at all the raving animal she had expected. She swallowed hard.

Ross was sweeping the area, the rifle following his eyes like a well-trained Labrador. He stopped once, listening, but there was no sound. It was like a graveyard, he thought. How apt!

His feet were kicking up the tiniest of dust clouds as he stepped through the wood chippings and crunched the fallen leaves.

He was so close now that Millie could almost reach out and touch him. She had been holding her breath for what seemed like forever, too afraid to exhale. But now she summoned up every ounce of strength and lunged forward, the large piece of timber she had found circling dangerously above her head. She screamed as she pounced and took some pleasure in the terrific thud as the wood struck flesh and bounced back in her hand, recoiling like a spring, ready for the next strike.

Ross went down in a heap, blood pumping from a wide gash in the side of his head, the skin already turning blue and ugly. He fired off the rifle but had no control of it, and the bullet whistled into the wind, separating the leaves in a nearby birch. As the weapon dropped from his grip, he reached out for her and managed to grab one arm. The lump of wood began to come down again, but this time he was ready, and he spun to his right, sensing the club harmlessly swing past his face. Despite himself, he grinned, and took a grip of Millie's other arm which held the wood, twisting it painfully until she could hold on no longer. As the club fell, so did Millie, tumbling down on top of Ross and knocking the wind out of him.

The impact forced him to release her, so she jumped to her feet and struggled to retrieve her club, her only salvation. But as her grip tightened around the wood, Ross stood up, with the rifle pointed at her. His finger was on the trigger, but he hesitated, a vision of Paulette clouding his judgement... and he was lost.

A volley of small-arms fire echoed from the edge of the wood as three agents emerged, each firing their 23s at eye level for maximum effect. Raymond Ross died the same way Bonnie and Clyde had done, and almost as messily.

****

Rafferty was out of puff and certainly out of condition, so it was with some relief that he stopped to answer his mobile phone. "Rafferty," he spluttered, giving the impression of someone making a heavy-breathing call.

The agent on the other end was a little perplexed at the sound of his boss, but, always the professional, he was brisk and to the point. "Patterson here, sir. We've got the girl, safe and well. One fatality on our side," he added, with a lump in his throat.

"Who?" asked Rafferty, who always dreaded this kind of conversation. It meant more paperwork, of course, but more than that, he felt deeply the loss of a colleague.

"Agent Abrahams, sir."

Rafferty nodded, even though Patterson couldn't see the gesture. Abrahams was so much like a younger Rafferty it hurt even more. When he had been shot all those years ago, it had resulted in only a slight limp. He thanked God every day for his life but hated the deity equally for taking the other agents from him. This was his family. "I'm sorry," he said limply.

Patterson understood. "Yes, sir." He paused. "We got the perp, sir."

"Safely in custody?"

"No, sir. In a body bag."

He knew it wasn't right, but Rafferty felt a modicum of satisfaction at the outcome. It wouldn't help Abrahams' family one iota, but the Service would take a grain of compensation from it. "Have you ID'd?"

"We believe it is Raymond Ross, you know, from the Mercurial Bank."

"Yes," said Rafferty, "I am sure it is." He closed his phone and put it back in his pocket, his heart heavy for a moment.

Finally, he looked up and saw his men standing there, watching him. The sad and good news could wait... it was time to go to war. "For the Service!" he bellowed, and his men were ready to follow him into the valley of death.

Chapter Thirty-Three

The General saw nothing out of place as Number Two came into the clearing with Lucas Black. He smiled wickedly in greeting them. "It is so nice to see you again, Lucas."

"His name is Ty now," Hector said, receiving just a scowl from his master.

Ty studied the other man. Very slightly stooped, no doubt due to the bullet in the back, but he looked just the same as he always had. Ty spat on the ground. "You butchered my friend," he said, his voice level, even if his ire was at full power.

"I did," the General said, so matter-of-factly that Ty spat on the ground again. The General ignored him. "Now, Lucas, what am I going to do with you? You deserve something special for what you did to me."

Ty thought about that one for a couple of seconds before replying. "What, you think I shot you?" He began to laugh. The General didn't like that one bit.

"What are you saying?" he demanded.

Ty couldn't contain himself. "You dumb-ass! Want to know who really shot you? It was Ralphie... you know, the one guy you *didn't* kill."

"I don't believe you!" screamed the General. But he did, and he was sickened that he had not taken out the man who had caused him so much pain. Not only that, but Lucas had deprived him of any chance of revenge he might have had. He was boiling, close to erupting.

Number Two tried to step away, but Ty had a firm grip round his throat. He raised his revolver and pointed it at the General. "So, the question is really, what am I going to do with you, Arsehole?"

The General sniggered. He had regained some composure, and at the same time had seen a change come over Lucas and was desperate not to let him see his own turmoil. "Really, Lucas, do you think you can kill me? I see only fear in your eyes. You are not like me. You are not capable. Your war exploits have left you brain-dead." He stepped to one side, levelling his machine-gun. There was also a pair of pistols in the waistband of his combat trousers, and a Bowie knife in a sheath strapped to his left leg. A one-man arsenal.

"If you open fire, *Ector* here will get the first burst. By then you will be dead yourself," said Ty, his voice controlled and measured.

The General threw back his head and laughed loudly. "Ha! Do you imagine I care about *him*? I can kill you both without even thinking about it."

Number Two was astounded at this statement and horrified that he meant so little to the man whose life he had saved. He mumbled something in Spanish and then cried out, "What are you saying, *General*?"

The General ignored him, instead focusing on Ty, who was almost imperceptibly rocking backwards and forwards, causing Hector to do the same. They made a strange sight, and the General was spellbound.

It was a stand-off, but one that the General was relishing. He could see the darkness growing within Lucas's eyes, the sweating and shaking that was starting to engulf his body. The General had studied his war record and subsequent descent into hell, before he had emerged, scarred and broken, after extensive therapy. The thought that Lucas had probably been suffering mentally all the time *he* had been enduring the physical pain from the bullet gave the General a warm feeling, and he smiled with satisfaction. "You will not pull the trigger, Lucas. I know it... and so do you."

Hector tried to look at Ty, but the grip round his throat was tight. "*Señor* Ty, do something," he whispered. "For both our sakes." He could feel the shakes coursing through Ty's body and was not sure how long the man would continue standing.

Ty could see nothing. His eyes had clouded so much that even the blurred image of the Arsehole had disappeared. All he heard was the raucous din of battle, the shouts and screams, the gunfire, the explosions. He was transported to the one place he never wanted to go back to, and there was nothing he could do about it. He felt himself swaying but had no control. The pistol was slipping from his grip, but he knew instinctively that he had to hold on to it – the enemy were close. It was going to be hand-to-hand. He wanted to wipe the sweat from his face, but he couldn't. He knew he had the gun in one hand, but where was his other hand? He tried to look, but it was useless. He could hear breathing, close by, and knew it wasn't his. The enemy? He squeezed his left hand and was rewarded with a gasp. He'd got one of them! All he had to do was pull the trigger, and he could move on to the next one. There were so many of them now…

"Drop the gun, Billy!"

Who said that? Who is Billy? Ty was ready to fire, but he needed to know more. What if the man he was holding was a friend? He loosened his grip and tried to focus.

The General swivelled at the sound of his name. To his amazement, there was a sheriff's deputy standing before him, gun aimed and cocked.

"I said drop it," the deputy repeated.

The General screamed and fired at the same time, moving to his left in case the deputy had the chance to reply. He didn't.

Dawg tumbled forward, clutching his leg. It hadn't been a killing shot, and the General was not happy about that. He cursed loudly, the sound adding confusion to Ty's already befuddled brain.

Ty, somehow, had fallen, the man he was holding having bounced off him and rolled away. Then the man was close by, whispering in his ear. What was he saying? Something about having to get out of there. "Come on, *señor!*" Yes, he understood that! "Run, run!" And he was up, rushing for his life, the pistol forgotten, even though it was still in his hand. He didn't like the idea of retreating, but sometimes it was the only sane thing to do. He sensed bullets zipping past his legs, the sound muffled in his addled brain as if he was playing a distant video game with no headset. Suddenly, his eyes were open, unclouded now, and he could see the building approaching, its protective walls reaching out for him. Then he was through the door, gasping and retching, the sound of battle completely gone, as if it had never been. Hector was beside him, and they stared at each other for long seconds, each catching their breath and coughing from the exertion. With an unspoken bond, both men made their way to the rear of the building, looking for freedom…

****

The General was about to fire off another burst, when a new voice called, "That's enough!"

Phil Lenier came into view from the left, followed by Sheriff Withers straight in front. The General had scurried behind a metal water butt, and quickly let off a round, the haphazard shots flying harmlessly between the officers, who were still well apart. The General had received no training in the use of the weapon he held, having been given it by Ray, who knew a man who knew a man. His lack of expertise showed in the hit-or-miss way he tried to replace the cartridge, dropping it once and scrambling for it, before hearing the satisfying click as it fell into place. He was ready.

Withers indicated for Lenier to move to the left, while he himself kept right. They were going to come round the back, or so they thought.

The General shifted position and saw what was happening. He slipped away from the water butt and found the sanctuary of some trees, which he sheltered behind, just as Lenier opened fire, the crackling shots hitting the butt and the ground behind the General's feet as he ran. He smiled when he realised that they had all missed, and he fired back with an abandon that made Lenier dive for cover in turn.

"Are you okay, Phil?" Withers shouted.

"Fine, boss," came the reply, although the voice was far from confident.

Withers had never experienced anything like this before. He had led such a sheltered life! He crouched behind a tree and looked out, seeing nothing. He listened. Nothing. A bird took flight, the noise of its flapping wings seemingly exaggerated in the otherwise peacefulness of the day. Withers was about to move on when he caught sight of something from the corner of his eye – a man, hobbling through the undergrowth towards the General's position. Dawg! Withers held his breath.

Lenier, too, had seen his colleague, and offered a silent prayer. Wounded or not, Dawg was going to see the job through. Lenier knew that he had to offer his support. He stretched his cramped legs as best he could, and sprang forward, heading for the next safe haven. The General spotted the movement and took aim. Lenier was a sitting target, and the General had no feelings either way as his finger depressed the trigger. A spray of death erupted from the machine-gun, and Phil Lenier fell into the bush that was going to be his salvation. As if in slow-motion, he rolled down the bush and onto the ground, the only sound being his last breath, escaping his body as he came to a halt, face-up, his blood staining his uniform and the ground in equal measure.

Dawg stopped dead, stunned. He fell on one knee and aimed, before firing two bullets at the General. There was a cry of pain and another burst of machine-gun fire in response, but Dawg had already gone to ground, safe.

"I think I got him, boss," he shouted with some delight. Like his sheriff, this was all new to him. Nothing ever happened in Bakerton.

The General tried to stem the flow of blood in his arm, and old thoughts began to go through his mind. The agony of a bullet wound was still raw in his memory, and this just added to his anger. He was going to kill the bastard for this!

Withers watched in horror as the General came out of his hiding place, gun poised at his hip, and began walking straight towards Dawg. The man seemed to have no fear, Withers thought, even as he raised his gun and fired. The bullet missed but unsettled a small flock of pigeons from the nearest tree, sent squawking to the skies in fright. Dawg also fired again, but the General seemed impervious to anything thrown at him. He sent a burst into the undergrowth where Dawg was sheltering and then turned towards Withers. The sheriff took aim once more, determined to finish this once and for all. He fired, and saw his enemy stop in his tracks, a look of pain etched on his face. Got you, Withers thought triumphantly, but then he saw flashes from the General's weapon and felt a strangely exquisite pain in his side as he fell backwards, hitting his head on the branch of a tree. As the gun slipped from his grip, he slid to the ground and looked through hazy, pain-soaked eyes as the General walked towards him. He thought of Lucas Black but knew he wouldn't be any help. He couldn't even see him. Probably dead already. Now it's my turn, he thought, without any desolation. It will only be a good thing…

****

As Withers groaned quietly, he saw Dawg lying on the ground some way away. He wasn't moving, but Withers sensed – or, rather, hoped – he was still alive. Withers tried to get up, but the bullet in his side seemed to roll with every movement, causing nausea to fill his chest and throat. He coughed, recoiling at the pain searing through him. He tried to pick up his gun and point it at his target. He knew he had passed out for a second and was surprised to find himself still alive.

He tried to turn at the sound of approaching footsteps, found his gun and watched through dim eyes as it hovered in mid-air, waving about uncontrollably. He held his breath and tried to balance the wayward weapon, gritting his teeth with sheer determination. He saw a shimmering figure getting closer, seemingly floating on air. His mind was beginning to play tricks with him, but his weak finger managed to grip the trigger tighter, and he used his other hand to steady his aim. He was ready.

Then, as if out of a mist, the General was standing above him, his wounded arm hanging by his side, but the machine-gun firmly gripped in the other hand, ready to deal out the final roll of the dice. He was grinning insanely. Withers knew he had to fire, but his fingers wouldn't work. It was all he could do to hold on to his pistol. He blinked, as if that might spirit the General away. It didn't. He was still there, leaning over the sheriff and toying with him. He raised his weapon and moved closer, aiming it at Withers' temple. "Between the eyes, sheriff," he said, that terrible grin creasing his face. "I've done it many times before. So easy."

Withers heard the words and waited for the inevitable bang. It came soon enough.

****

He didn't understand. Looking straight ahead, he could still see the prostrate Dawg – but where was the General? He flexed his fingers and reached out again for his fallen gun, his hands scrabbling around until he found it and, with renewed strength he didn't realise he had, he brought the gun up, moving it in an arc as his eyes studied the whole area. Someone was coming towards him... getting closer. He was ready to fire.

"Hold on there, partner!"

Withers winced as another wave of pain hit him. Did he recognise the voice? He licked his dry lips and took aim once more.

Then, suddenly, the man was kneeling beside him, gently taking the gun from his hand and easing his head back onto the ground. Withers had no strength to argue. If this was the end, then so be it.

"Take it easy, John. It's Pat. I'm on your side, remember?"

Pat? How the hell did he get here? Withers found his voice, although he didn't recognise it. "Dawg! Help Dawg."

"My men are already on it, John," soothed Rafferty, holstering his own gun and taking off his jacket to lay it under the head of the delirious sheriff. "It's all under control."

Withers began to relax and allowed Rafferty to tend his wound. He was in a no-man's-land of make-believe, where mixed messages ran through his mind and tingles ran through his body. He twisted his head to the side... and came face to face with the sightless eyes of the General lying beside him.

Chapter Thirty-Four

Five days later, Withers was sitting up in a hospital bed, a pretty little nurse fussing around him. Judith sat in a chair next to him, looking just like the cat who'd got the cream. She smiled as Withers tried to shoo away the nurse, without success: she had a job to do, and no ornery sheriff was going to stop her. Finally, she tucked in the bottom of the sheet, gave him a withering but at the same time comforting look, and left.

As the door closed, it was thrown open again by the arrival of Rafferty, a bag of grapes in his hand.

"Didn't know what to bring the invalid," he said, placing the bag on the bed.

"Pizza? Mama's own cheesecake?" pleaded Withers, knowing the answer without looking. "Thanks, Pat. At least someone's looking after my figure."

"Truth be told," Rafferty admitted, "they were Kitty Janowski's idea. I've just come from her and Dawg's place."

Withers looked up. "How is he?"

"He's fine, John. Amazingly, the General only got him with the one bullet – it broke a bone on the way through his leg. He eventually passed out, which was probably the thing that saved his life. He's got a plaster cast on it now. Hobbles around like Chester Goode." When Judith gave him a quizzical look, he added, "From the old *Gunsmoke* TV show" – but she still didn't have a clue. Rafferty didn't pursue the subject. "Millie Moody's out of hospital and on the mend. Just suffering from shock. My men got to her just in time." He looked pensive. "Shame we had to lose two fine colleagues, though, John."

As Rafferty's thoughts dwelled on Agent Abrahams, Withers couldn't quite believe that Phil Lenier had fallen in the line of duty. He looked serious. "I owe you, Pat."

"Nuts!"

"You killed the General and saved my life out there – and Dawg's. But how did you know where we were? We didn't keep you in the loop," he added sheepishly.

Rafferty grinned. "I was always with you, John."

"What, you tailed me?"

"Not so much tailed – more *supported*. I was under instructions to let you run with the case, but to keep an eye on you. I've been almost everywhere you have. I was behind you when you went to see Grace Templeman and Paul Cassidy."

"I didn't know," said Withers.

"That's because I'm a special agent!" Both men laughed. "The only time you caught me out was that stunt you pulled with Vincent Pandando. I never saw that one coming."

"Sorry about that."

"No problem. My men swooped in and pulled him off the island a while ago. He's helping us with our inquiries – from the inside of a prison cell, this time!" Rafferty paused, letting it all sink in. He saw Withers grimace with pain and felt for his friend. "So, what's your prognosis?" he asked, keen to change the subject.

"Another week in here, they say. Then it's a spell of convalescing. Those kind people at the Mercurial have offered me Ralph Baxter's old place up on the Ridge free of charge for a while."

"Sounds like a deal," said Rafferty. "You may get to see that picture of the lovely Salome again."

"I can't wait."

Rafferty turned to Judith. "You're looking positively sparkling this morning. Pleased your boyfriend is on the mend, I assume."

"Well, yes, of course," said Judith with a wide smile. "But it's even better than that."

Withers gave her a pained look. "What's better than me?"

"I finally got myself the scoop of the year, that's all." She waited for them to gush. They didn't. "You took the Raymond Ross story from me," she said pointedly, looking at Withers. "But yesterday, I got mail. Telling the whole story. Everything."

Finally, Withers bit. "Okay, we're listening."

"Tomorrow morning, the *Altona Oracle* will publish the truth about the Figgis killings. From the man on the inside."

"What?" both men said.

"Yes, Ty Cobden – sorry, your Lucas Black – has told me everything."

"He's alive!" gasped Withers, feeling the pain in his side. He gave Rafferty a homicidal look. "You let him go, *again*, Pat!"

Rafferty recoiled from the sudden onslaught. "Careful, buddy, don't go stretching your sutures. Listen, my immediate concern was saving your scrawny neck, which I did. I left my men to clear up the other mess…"

"And they didn't!" gasped Withers, exasperated.

"It was the heat of battle, John. It was like the OK Corral out there!"

Withers cooled. "Yeah, I suppose." He sank back on his bed, suddenly exhausted. "Thanks, Wyatt," he finally said with a watery grin. Rafferty just raised a hand and gave the merest of salutes.

"When you two have finished..." Judith burst into their bubble, hands on hips and wearing the sternest of faces. They looked at her. "I've got this world exclusive, and all you can do is fight like little children." Her stare was so powerful that both men quivered and fell deathly silent. But she just couldn't hold it any longer and dissolved into laughter, the others soon joining in.

Withers had to stop before he did himself some permanent damage. He was suddenly serious. "So, where is he?" he demanded.

"Don't know. Just got the letter. Posted out of town."

"You do know he's wanted for the killing of Ralph Baxter?" Withers was getting agitated again, and Rafferty put a hand on his shoulder to calm him. None of them wanted his wound to explode along with his temper.

Judith looked him square in the eye. "He also led you to the General. And he just wants to clear the name of his friend Leroy. What's so bad about that? I guess he sent the letter because an email could have been traced. He's not stupid, you know!"

Withers and Rafferty exchanged looks. "That he isn't," agreed Withers. And he also knew something else for certain: this story wasn't finished yet.